THE ENDURANCE

NATHAN SMITH

Fire and Ice F|
a young adult imprint of Melange Books, LLC

1

EVERY MUTINY NEEDS MUTINEERS

WAVES ROCK THE SPANISH WARSHIP. THE LANTERN CASTS A SHADOW across the crate of oranges that sent me tumbling. I reach for a piece of fruit before it rolls away, but a hand reaches down, hooks my arm, and pulls me up with the momentum of the boat. The boy brushes off my shoulder. He holds the lantern to my face to make sure I'm not too scuffed up. A girl of seventeen has her legs dangling over a crate, watching us. Her soiled yellow dress is like a wilted sunflower in the brig of the pirate vessel, the *San Paulo*.

The three of us are the sole occupants of this dripping cell. They want to escape as much as I do. All we need is a plan. For, with a clever enough plan, one man—or a lad of sixteen years—could depose a pirate captain.

We may be hunkered in a musty brig with no light save our little lantern. The waterlogged walls may creak. Our bunks may be damp with rot. But we have an opportunity. An opportunity in need of a clever plan.

It just so happens that I have a very clever plan.

Crafty as my plan may be, I cannot steal an entire pirate ship by myself. Much less sail it. Every mutiny needs mutineers.

Now to enlighten them of the opportunity.

"Tonight, we can break out of here, steal this ship, and then steal enough gold to sit high and pretty for a dozen lifetimes, but there'll be no going back. No matter what happens, we can never show our faces in civilized, or uncivilized, society again. We'll have to disappear somewhere remote. Africa maybe. I need to know if you're both completely committed."

The girl narrows her eyes, but leans in. She's skeptical yet intrigued.

The boy has his feet planted against the rocking ship, arms crossed. He chews his bottom lip and intently studies the stream of water sloshing across the floor. He's obviously considering my proposal.

"Well?" I prod.

He looks up. His hair is dark brown and held back from his eyes by a ratty bandana. He's small for sixteen. A torn brown vest covers his grimy tunic. His chin is hairless, but lantern light reflects fire in his eyes.

"I'm in."

He was the ship's cabin boy. Back when I was the only prisoner of the *San Paulo*—and before he got tossed in here with me—he'd come visit. We're the same age. He liked my company and, truth be told, he didn't have any friends among the crew.

"How do I know I can trust you?"

"If Captain Rodriguez hadn't thrown me in here with you, you couldn't."

Rodriguez de Medina is the soon-to-be-previous captain of the *San Paulo*. He's an odd mix—a violent madman and a devout Catholic. Well, as devout a Catholic as you can be and still be a pirate. At least devout enough to name his ship the *San Paulo*. He wanted to name it *El Ángel*, but the crew nearly mutinied. So, he settled for naming it after a saint.

When the British Navy knocked-off Blackbeard, Rodriguez took up the mantle of the most feared pirate in the Caribbean. I won't mention how many ships he's taken or the fortunes he's won. It would take far too long.

Only fools aren't afraid of him and the influence he wields among outlaws. Every pirate between Nassau and Barcelona knows and respects Captain Rodriguez de Medina.

That's why, after stealing his ship, we'll have no place in uncivilized society.

"Rodriguez threw me down here with the likes of you because I spilt his ink. I have no love for the captain," Charlie says.

The answer to my question is obvious—I can trust Charlie because he hates Captain Rodriguez.

It's the girl's turn.

Her eyes are still fixed on me, ready for me to get on with the plan.

"And you, princess? Are you in?"

"I'm no princess. I'm the daughter of a governor," she corrects me.

Her name is Isabelle. She's a Spaniard kissed by the sun because she refused to stay away from the ocean. Her skin is nearly as dark as mine. If I didn't know better, I'd say she was mixed blood, like me. I've got the skin of a light African, but the green eyes of an Englishman—a blend that never ceases to irritate the white man.

Charlie is a scorned urchin from a scorned port town no one has ever heard of. Isabelle, however, is the daughter of the Governor of Havana.

She has power from her family name, and from the make of her soul. Some people wield power like a sword they were born holding. She's one of those people. She makes you believe her head was meant to wear a crown.

Other people, like me, have to wrestle power from the cold, dead hands of men like Captain Rodriguez.

I overheard Captain Rodriguez's plan to ransom her. The Governor is willing to pay a fortune to get Isabelle back. But Rodriguez has other items on his agenda. He didn't plan on ransoming Isabelle until he took the British treasure ship, the *Endurance*.

The *Endurance* has more treasure in it than the New World has ever seen in one place, and it's on its way to London. It'd be a shame to pirates everywhere if it arrived unmolested.

The *Endurance* presents a rare opportunity. Never has a ship so laden with treasure sailed past grimy pirate hands. Even Rodriguez can't muster a prize much larger than a load of sugar stolen from traders leaving the colonies. The *Endurance* carries more loot than Blackbeard could have amassed given four lifetimes.

And soon, it'll be mine.

Isabelle is crucial to the plan. We need a third conspirator. But she's a liability no matter which way you slice it. Either the governor's men will come looking for her, or she'll try to turn us in before we take the *Endurance*.

"Yes or no?" I ask.

"Let me hear your plan. Then I'll decide."

She's a smart one, wants to see all your cards before she'll commit any of hers. Calculating.

I want her to realize the magnitude of my plan. "There'll be no going back, even if we fail. We'll spend the rest of our lives in some uncivilized place, the lords of great treasure, but hidden nonetheless. You'll never be able to go back home."

"I've got nothing to go home to."

That's probably the best I'll get from her. I motion for them to come close. "My name is James." They should know the creator's name—the god of this genesis of immense treasure. "How many crewmen do you two think are currently left on board?"

Isabelle leans in, eyes wide—she sees where I'm going. She admires the boldness of the plan. "No more than four. The rest are on the beach."

Now you see the opportunity we've been presented.

All that stands between us and ownership of the *San Paulo* are four pirates.

The rest of the crew is on the beach, partying around a bonfire, relaxing before their date with the *Endurance* tomorrow evening.

The *San Paulo* is anchored in a remote bay. No port cities around for miles. If we run off with the ship, Captain Rodriguez and his crew will be marooned.

"We dispose of the crewmen currently aboard, and we take the *San Paulo*." I lean back and let them consider my proposal.

Isabelle chuckles. "Even if we could somehow throw those poor saps overboard, and then, by some miracle of God, sail this ship out of the bay, what will we do with a stolen pirate ship? Become pirates ourselves?"

"Yes." My eyes lock with hers and I think she wants to smile. "That's the plan, but we won't be pirates for long. Only a few days. My plan has three stages. Stage one, we dispose of the four crewmen and steal the *San Paulo*. Stage two, we move into position to relieve the *Endurance* of her treasure. Captain Rodriguez has her course marked on the map. Correct, Charlie?"

Charlie nods in the gloomy dark—a conspirator's night. "Aye. Before he threw me down here, I saw the map and the *Endurance*'s expected position. The map is tucked away in his study. His plan was to take the *Endurance*'s gold and then sail for Havana to ransom Isabelle."

"You won't be ransoming me," Isabelle says, her voice unyielding as iron.

A simple enough request. "Alright, we'll drop you off wherever—"

"No, you'll take me with you to Africa."

"Fine. Africa. There, that's settled. Which brings us to stage three: we sail the ship across the Atlantic and find a remote settlement in Africa. Somewhere that won't question why three adolescents have the treasure of a king. And then we'll live out the rest of our days, counting gold, drinking rum, and napping in the sun."

Charlie grins. He's sold.

But Isabelle—she's shaking her head. "Your plan is truly brilliant," she whispers sarcastically. "We'll be the richest Europeans on the African content, but the *San Paulo* isn't a small sloop. How will we sail a three-mast warship?"

I hadn't fully considered the how of the plan yet. How hard could it be? I pride myself in simple deviousness. I brush her concerns away with a wave of my hand. "Sailing a ship is easy. You just drop some sails and point her in the right direction. And besides, Charlie is an expert. He studied under the great Captain Rodriguez. He knows how to sail the *San Paulo*. Isn't that right, Charlie?"

"I read a book on sea navigation once."

"See, an expert." I pat Charlie's shoulder.

"You can't be serious. There's no way. And anyway, if we do somehow manage to sail the *San Paulo*, what will we do when we encounter the *Endurance*? Do you expect her to just give you her treasure?"

I smile. This is the best part of the plan. "That's exactly what I expect. She'll hand it right over. Charlie, when was the last time the *San Paulo* engaged in combat?"

"If we hadn't had a rumble with Captain Marcelo and the *Damascus* a few weeks ago, it would have been nearly a year. But we shouldn't count that. Rodriguez and Marcelo are old rivals and can't resist crossing swords. No cargo ships have put up a fight in eight months."

"Exactly. Ships don't fight Captain Rodriguez anymore. He is the most feared pirate in the Caribbean. His reputation, not his cannons, beat his prey into submission. Opposing captains surrender. They know they don't stand a chance. We'll use Rodriguez's reputation to rob the *Endurance*. We'll sail Captain Rodriguez's ship, fly Captain Rodriguez's flag, and the *Endurance* will think we're Captain Rodriguez and they'll lay down."

"And if they don't?" Isabelle asks. "If they put up a fight?"

"They won't," I say, hoping it's true.

A silent moment passes.

"Well?" I ask.

"I was sold five minutes ago. I'm in," Charlie says.

Isabelle is silent. She's obviously turning the thoughts in her head, calculating our chances. She doesn't want to go back home, that much is obvious, but I can't understand why. Why would you leave a life of wealth?

Her lips purse. "Not only does your plan require the three of us to perform impossible tasks, like sailing a warship by ourselves, it puts us in danger of pirate hunters. What if we're sailing along and bump into Captain Solway of the *London Wolf*? We're near the Fortress of Long Rock —Solway patrols these waters. You've heard stories about what he does to pirates. What if he catches us? What if we hit a storm? What if the *Endurance* isn't ready to hand over her gold? What if—"

"We can't control the 'what ifs.' All we can control are the actions we take. We can take the *San Paulo* and we can sail it. We'll have to take the rest as it comes. If you're still unsure, I'll flip you for it."

From my pocket I pull an old, dented Spanish doubloon.

It's my lucky coin.

Isabelle likes to plan her moves, carefully plotting each detail so that she wins. Yet I think she also enjoys the thrill of chance.

"Alright," she says.

I hold up the doubloon, showing them the Spanish king's face. "Heads, we break out of the brig and steal the *San Paulo*. Tails, we forget this mad plan."

"Toss it," Isabelle says.

I flip the coin.

To them, it spins through the air like a star aligning to determine our destiny. To me, I see the day my father gave it to me. I barely came up to his hip then. That day, I followed him to where he worked—the British fortress in Barbados.

As we walked, men mocked him and the color of my skin. *"Finally got yourself a slave boy there, did you, Captain Higgins?"*

At the fortress dock, my father's men were chipping barnacles from a ship under his command. I jabbered about how strong a ship was. Nothing could hurt something so big. Finally, he held out a small, insignificant Spanish doubloon. "What do you see?"

"Why do you have Spanish money?" I asked.

"Never mind that." He tossed me the coin. "Break it."

I bent fiercely but nothing happened. I bit and clawed and banged the doubloon on the dock, but I didn't leave a scratch.

"Here," my father said. He took a hammer from one of his soldiers. I handed back the doubloon. With the hammer, he laid one blow to the indestructible coin. It bent in half. He held it up. "Everything, even the strongest vessel, breaks with the right leverage. Especially when it doesn't see it coming."

With a final blow from the hammer, he knocked the coin into its original shape. He gave it to me. The lesson, and the luck, stuck to the coin in my pocket. It has always landed on—

"Heads," Charlie says as I reveal the coin.

Isabelle nods. "Okay, I'll help, but your plan is terrible, full of holes. We'll need to make some serious adjustments at stage two."

"One thing at a time. We've got a ship to take, but first we need to get out of this cell."

"How are we going to do that? I don't suppose you have a key?" Isabelle asks.

"Nope. We have you."

I wink at her. I shift my eyes to the half-drunk pirate on the other side of the wooden prison bars.

He's supposed to be guarding us, but instead he's leaned back in an old chair. Slobber runs down his face; matted hair covers his head. He's nearly asleep—enjoying having the quiet ship to himself. The ship won't be quiet for long.

Poor sap has no idea what's coming.

2

COMMANDEERING THE SAN PAULO

ISABELLE PROPS HERSELF ON HER ELBOW AND BLOWS HAIR OUT OF her face. Her legs are contorted before the door. An orange rolls into the leg that's supposedly broken, as to lure in the guard. There's plenty for a young lady to trip on down here. And we all heard Rodriguez's order to keep her safe. She grunts and sits up. "This is never going to work."

Charlie and I are bundled up in our bunks, pretending to be asleep. But Charlie's foot pokes out from his blanket. He's got it propped on a tower of poorly stacked orange crates. It's teetering with the ship's sway, begging to tip over and break someone's leg.

"Lay back down. It'll work," I whisper. "Remember, Isabelle, damsel in distress. We knock over these crates, you look like you've hurt your leg. Charlie and I won't stir so he'll think we're still asleep. Just act hurt and helpless."

"And show a little more leg," Charlie says.

I reach down from my bunk and punch Charlie's shoulder. He and I suppress laughter.

"I hate you both." Isabelle hikes her dress up to her knees, puts on a pained but sultry face, and gives Charlie the signal.

He kicks over the stack of crates. The wood plats shatter against the floor, oranges roll everywhere, and the old pirate stutters. "Wha—No,

Captain, I swear I was watching— Oh. It's just you three making a racket. Quiet down!"

"Help, help," Isabelle says, "I've hurt my leg and I need help."

The pirate rubs his face. A fresh swig of rum sloshes in his mouth. He puts his hand on his knee and pushes himself from his chair. He wobbles with each crashing wave and braces himself against the ship's support beams. But he doesn't drop his bottle of rum.

"Well, are you going to stand there like a stupid tree or help me? I mean—thank goodness, you're here. I think I've hurt my poor little leg…"

He's drunk enough to forget that he is horribly ugly—with a hunched back, grime coated skin, and yellowed eyes—and that Isabelle is exceedingly beautiful. He forgets that pretty girls never ask creepy old men for help.

He scratches his head and gestures to me and Charlie with the bottle of rum. "How're those two boys still asleep after all this ruckus?"

Isabelle shrugs. "Hard sleepers, maybe."

"Aye, hard sleepers." He turns to Isabelle. "Well, we best make sure your little arm isn't hurt, shouldn't we?"

"My leg."

"Ah, your leg."

The pirate fumbles the ring of keys from his belt. As he clinks through the keys, Isabelle casts me a glance. I nod. Charlie and I are ready when the door clicks open.

The pirate staggers into the cell, blunders on an orange, and spits a curse. As he steadies, he drops his bottle of rum. The rolling bottle clinks into Charlie's cot. Silently, Charlie reaches from under his blanket, grabs the heavy bottle, and pulls it into the folds of his bed.

Isabelle scoots back, bringing the pirate deeper into the room. She scowls at me. *Get on with it before he has the chance to examine my leg.*

The old pirate passes the threshold of the cell door. He shows Charlie and I his back. Charlie rises from his bunk. He tests the rum bottle's weight by slapping it into his open palm. The creaking ship masks the smacks.

"Now," I whisper.

"Huh?" The pirate swings around.

Charlie slams the glass bottle over the pirate's head. He thumps to the floor in a bloody mess. His hair is sticky with blood. His eyes are wide with anger at his own stupidity. He calls for help, but Charlie dives to cover his mouth. The old pirate squirms to push Charlie off. But Charlie keeps him pinned.

I take the curved dagger from the pirate's belt. "Let's end this."

"Wait, you're going to kill him?" Charlie asks.

Under Charlie's hold, the pirate struggles. The dagger reflects in the pirate's panicked eyes.

"What did you expect?" I snap. "That we'd extend the right hand of fellowship to him? That he would join our little mutiny and help us steal the treasure from the *Endurance*?"

"Well, I dunno. I just thought we could throw him overboard or something?"

"And let him swim back to shore and tell the captain that three runts are stealing the *San Paulo*?" I say.

"Tie him up. He won't be able to swim so quick," Isabelle suggests.

The pirate's eyes dart between the three of us as we argue about whether or not to kill him. Intermingled with the anger and fear is utter disbelief.

"That will kill him just as much as putting a dagger in his chest." Charlie grows tired of the pirate's struggling and slams his head against the floor.

"It'll be hard for him, but he can struggle his way to shore or he can choose to drown. That's the best anyone can ask for. Tie him up. We'll throw him over once we get the others," I say.

I hand Isabelle a dirty sock. She deserves the honor of stuffing it in the pirate's mouth to gag him.

Charlie straddles the pirate and ties his arms and legs. We stash him under the bunks. I swipe the ring of keys from his belt. Might need these later. He squirms around, but I dull his thumping by stuffing heavy boxes under with him.

He's not going anywhere.

———

Our shadows pass over the hammocks strung between the support beams. The hull is empty. Quiet as three spooks, we duck beneath ropes, climb over cannons, and keep our heads low. Whether it's a loud creaking, footsteps, or a suspicious light, I stop our party at any sign of the crew still aboard the *San Paulo*.

"James, we should raid the storeroom before going above deck." Charlie nods toward a heavy door.

We best arm ourselves before facing any pirates. I have the dagger I took from our guard. But a knife only does so much against a pistol. I motion for us to make for the storeroom.

The stolen keys clink as I find the one that unlocks the door. After a few tries, the door screeches open. I cringe and check over my shoulder. A whole horde of pirates must have heard that. All that's behind me is my shadow.

You'd think Rodriguez planned to wage war on the whole world. I run my hand over a row of rifles like they're the bars of a wrought iron fence. Charlie whistles as he counts the swords racked down the middle of the room. Beneath the rows of rifles are pistols on a bench, boxes of ammunition, and kegs of gun powder.

While Charlie and I are gawking, Isabelle straps on a weapon belt with a pistol, dagger, and cutlass. I've never seen a shark more comfortable in water than she is in that weapon belt.

She draws the sword and tests its weight. "Okay, lets go."

I grab a sheathed cutlass and slide it into my belt. Then I take two pistols from the bench and toss one to Charlie. "You'll be climbing the mast to let down the sails, but it never hurts to have a pistol. And you'll need this to cut the ropes." I give him my dagger.

He sheaths the dagger. But he holds the pistol like it's a demon trying to nip at his hand. Cabin boys don't usually fight. I pat his shoulder. "Steady, Charlie. No treasure was ever won without a little danger."

He looks me in the eye and stills himself. "Aye, Captain."

Isabelle stands by the door, impatiently keeping watch. "Are you two ready yet?"

"Yes," I say.

I turn from Charlie, crouch down, and move toward the hatch leading to the main deck. We haven't seen any crew; that means they're up there. Moonlight streaks through the hatch grate in dusty bands. I climb the ladder to peek through and survey the deck. The moon glows white and a cool breeze blows. It's a good night for mutiny. The full moon will cast shadows for young assassins.

Two pirates lean over the railing of the ship. They longingly look toward the beachside bonfire. Not only did they miss the party, they're about to take a swim. And then face the rage of Captain Rodriguez for losing his ship.

A third man's legs dangle from the crow's nest. He'll have a whistle. All three must be eliminated simultaneously to avoid alerting the horde of pirates on the beach.

I step back from the hatch and whisper, "Which sail needs to be opened to get us under way?"

Charlie licks his finger and sticks it through the grating to test the wind. "The main mast should be enough to get us going. I'll climb up there and set it loose. I'll add more sail once we're under way. We have the night wind. It's a straight shot to the open ocean. They'll never catch us."

"Good, you'll do that. Isabelle, can you handle the lookout in the crow's nest?"

She takes the dagger from her belt and clenches it between her teeth. She's ready to climb.

"I'll deal with the two chatting by the railing. Isabelle, you go first. Throw the guy from the crow's nest over. As soon as Isabelle disposes of the lookout, Charlie will drop the sails."

Charlie nods.

I lift the hatch. It squeaks open, but you can't hear it—not over the sea that's churning like my stomach. First Isabelle crawls out, then Charlie, then me. Isabelle and Charlie climb the rigging like silent devils. I move into position to toss my two pirates overboard.

I stop and hide in the shadow of the main mast. I smell the rum on their breath. They've been having their own party aboard the ship. Now how do I throw these two loggerheads off? I suppose I could slash the back of their legs and then—

A shrill whistle rips through the night. The lookout.

On the beach, a hundred pirates turn their heads toward the ship like a horde of monguls. The shore is silent save the sound of the crackling fire. Every man cranes his neck to hear the ship's disturbance. Some set down their mutton and stand. The undeniable figure of Captain Rodriguez rises before the fire. Rodriguez shouts, "To the boats! Something is amiss on my ship."

The pirates rush to the beached jolly boats, dash them into the water, and then cast themselves aboard. Too many men. Too many boats. We'll never make it if they board the *San Paulo*.

"Charlie, drop the sails now!" I yell.

My two pirates turn from the railing. They look at me in disbelief and draw their cutlasses. I take my pistol and cock it. They stop. I can't shoot them both, but one of them is going to die. And they're not ready to flip the coin to find out who.

The main sail drops in a flutter of moon glow and catches wind. The ropes taut and I stagger back. My finger grazes the trigger as the ship jolts. My pistol fires harmlessly into the night.

My pirate prey rush me. I draw my cutlass and block their strikes. I slash and cut the air, but not them. One of them knocks the blade from my hand and kicks my stomach, forcing me back. With no time to reload my pistol, I'm weaponless.

They back me up against the ship's cabin wall and laugh. "Wait till the captain gets a look at this. Little James here trying to steal the *San Paulo*."

The other man laughs. "I always liked James, but the poor boy doesn't ever think things all the way through."

The shrill whistle is replaced by a falling man's screams. The lookout hits the water with a crack. My two assailants turn to the sound of the splash. "We'll fish him out later."

"Aye, fish him out later. You think the captain wants James dead or alive?"

"Dead probably. He usually wants 'em dead."

The two pirates turn back to me, swords raised.

I'm done.

Well, it was a clever plan.

I force my eyes into a hard stare and steady my trembling lip.

"James, get down!" Isabelle swings on a rope from the crow's nest, her dress flapping like a warrior's cape, her eyes fixed on the heads of the two pirates. The heels of her shoes nail both of them across the temple. She tumbles on top of the limp men. Their heads are sticky with gushing blood. Her heel caved in one man's eye socket. He'll lose that eye.

I throw up.

"Some pirate you're turning out to be. Quick, toss them over," she says.

I wipe my mouth and help Isabelle drag the men to the railing of the ship. Charlie climbs down from the mast and joins us.

"Charlie, take the helm. Get us underway. They're coming," I say.

He runs for the bridge of the *San Paulo*.

We've almost done it. We've almost stolen the ship of the most infamous pirate in the Caribbean.

"Help me, you dunce!" Isabelle heaves the first man over the side of the ship. Bullets from the pirate laden jolly boats splinter into the ship. "And keep your head down!"

We lug the men overboard without getting shot to pieces. Isabelle's victim with the bloody eye wasn't so lucky.

The ship lurches and throws me against the railing. The sails are full, but the ship isn't moving. We're dead in the water.

"What just happened?" I ask.

Isabelle slams her palm against her forehead. "The anchor! We forgot about the bloody anchor."

The jolly boats glide like pond striders skidding across a lake. We've got to get moving or they'll storm the ship.

"James, we've stopped moving. We're at the end of the anchor chain," Charlie calls down from the bridge. "What're your orders?"

"Cut the chain!"

"Aye." Charlie jumps from the bridge of the ship with a large ax.

Isabelle runs to the weapon box on deck and takes two rifles. "How's your aim?"

No place for displays of manliness here. "Not the best."

"You load. I'll shoot. We don't have to shoot them all, just slow them down until Charlie cuts us free."

Loading the rifles would be easier if my hands weren't shaking and my heart wasn't pounding. I ram down the musket ball—and my fear—with the ramrod. I hand Isabelle the loaded rifle.

She lays it on the railing to steady her aim and cocks the hammer.

"Aim for Rodriguez," I say.

She pulls the trigger. The flash pan pops and the rifle booms. The man standing next to Rodriguez falls out of the jolly boat.

We duck beneath the railing to avoid the barrage of musket balls and curses.

I hand her the next loaded rifle. Charlie's ax clunks, the chain cracks. It's gulped down by the ocean. The ship lurches beneath our feet.

I stagger, but Isabelle retains her footing. She doesn't even have to readjust her aim. She keeps the rifle steady on the jolly boats and fires.

"Rifle." She holds out her hand—her eyes not blinking from her target—but I'd gotten distracted and hadn't reloaded the next one.

"Sorry."

The ship picks up speed. Charlie darts past us and calls over his shoulder, "James, new captain of the *San Paulo*, which way?"

"To sea!"

I look over the railing toward the jolly boats. They can't keep up. I flinch when the guns crack, but they're too far away. The bullets ping into the waves. Isabelle doesn't bother returning fire. Instead, she runs back to the rifle box, takes out a spy glass, and turns it toward the jolly boats. "Look at this."

She hands me the spyglass and I look across the black water to see Captain Rodriguez standing at the helm of his jolly boat, cursing into the wind, shaking one fist to God, and calling for another loaded pistol with the other. We did it. Three adolescents stole the ship of the most feared pirate in the world.

I look at Captain Rodriguez one more time. Somehow, he catches my eye through the telescope and examines my soul. He marks my features, so he will recognize me when the day comes for his revenge.

There'll be a reckoning for this.

But for tonight, I'm the new captain of the *San Paulo*.

3

THE PIRATE HUNTER

OUR GLASS BOTTLES CLINK. WE LAUGH INTO THE WARM CARIBBEAN night. Charlie props one hand on the spoked wheel, but there's no need. He's got it roped off to keep us sailing straight. The wind tousles his hair held back by a bandana. And he—the new helmsman of the *San Paulo*— has his eyes fixed on the star speckled horizon. He likes standing at the helm. It makes him feel good. Like he's a better pirate than he actually is. But now that I consider it, he and I are exceptional pirates. I've never heard of anyone stealing a ship with a three man crew.

I like standing on the bridge of the *San Paulo* too. One day, I'll have a go at the wheel, but Charlie can enjoy it for the night. Looking across the deck that stretches beyond the lantern light, lost in a haze of sea mist, and knowing it's all mine, is plenty for me.

The beach and Captain Rodriguez are far behind us. So Charlie and I crack open another crate of rum. We chuck half-full bottles into the sea before grabbing another. No need to be sparing—there's nearly as much food aboard the ship as there is armament. And there's a lot of armament.

"I know just what this night needs." Charlie tosses his rum bottle and disappears into the captain's cabin. A few moments later, he climbs the stairs to the bridge holding a violin.

The captain had insisted Charlie learn. The crew needed

entertainment. However, the crew enjoyed rum and women far more than Mozart. So, Charlie usually played only to himself.

He rosins the bow and then sets it against the strings. He fiddles it until music comes out. He may know his Mozart, but Charlie prefers lively tunes. The two of us dance and sing old tavern songs to the sea.

After a while, the music stops. Charlie sets down his violin, leans against the railing, catches his breath, and peels an orange. "Do you realize we just stole the ship of the most notorious pirate in the New World? Three kids. That was brilliant."

"Aye." I chuck another bottle into the limitless sea.

The ship sways. The waves beat against the hull. Sails flap, the rigging creaks, and the air is mixed with salt and freedom. The wind tugs at my clothes and I'm content. I could ask for nothing more.

Except perhaps a hull full of treasure.

I've spent many nights thinking about a moment like this. Though I never imagined I'd see it as a pirate captain. Before taking Rodriguez's ship, I'd never considered becoming a pirate. But I like the way the captain's boots fit. Could I be a pirate for the rest of my life? No. But for a few days it'll be fun.

When I ran away from home, I wanted to escape and gain riches. Only enough to set me up well for the rest of my life. I ran away from Barbados, stowed away on a smugglers ship bound for Nassau. When we arrived, I heard that Captain Rodriguez was anchored there.

My plan was to steal a bit of treasure from his stores, but one of his men caught me.

They locked me up. Captain Rodriguez needed time to decide what to do with me. He must've been taking a long time to decide. I was in the brig for a week before he dumped Isabelle and Charlie in there with me.

I now realize the flaw of my initial plan—it wasn't ambitious enough. I was thinking too small. The world is full of small thinkers.

The powers that be—the Rodriguezs, the British Crown, the Spanish Navy—they expect the small thinkers to make their small plans to steal small bits of treasure. They have contingencies for dealing with these nuisances. What they don't consider are the big schemers with ostentatious plans.

We successfully stole a notorious pirate's ship because of the audacity of our plan—its grit. We'll steal the largest British treasure in the New World for the same reason. No one will see us coming.

"And this ship. She handles beautifully." Charlie caresses the wheel. While I've been thinking, Charlie has been talking. I rejoin the one-sided conversation.

"Don't get too attached. We'll have to scuttle her when this is all done."

"Scuttle her?" He looks hurt. "Why? Why not just keep her?"

"By the end of this, we'll have made enemies of both Great Britain and the entire pirate world. We can't go on riding a stolen horse."

This might be the *San Paulo*—a prized ship—but in the end, it's just a ship.

"I guess you're right. But you'll have to light the match when the day comes. I don't think I can make myself do it. She's just too pretty of a boat." He taps the railing and turns his gaze from the horizon to me. "Hey, James, where'd you get this crazy idea? And not just that—I've been thinking, and I have lots of questions. What was a guy like you doing in a pirate brig? You're obviously educated. Your family has got money, surely."

"I saw the opportunity to take the *San Paulo* when I realized that the crew was going to be ashore that night." But he's right—there's more to the story. I'm more educated than I have the right to be. And I can read —a rarity among seamen.

I've read the works of military tacticians—ancient texts of conquest and riches. Any of the great men who ever lived—Alexander, Caesar, Mark Antony—they saw the opportunity their era presented and snatched it. You can't read about them without wanting to become them.

"Coming up with this plan was like walking the beach with my father, looking for shells. You could see them beneath the surf, but you had to grab them quick before the sea carried them away."

"You're a poet as well. Maybe you can write me a sonnet to give to Isabelle." He smiles as he thinks of her.

You don't find many women of Isabelle's caliber. She's a Cleopatra, or a Joan of Arc. "I don't believe she's the type who's interested in sonnets."

Isabelle steps onto the bridge, wearing fresh clothes and an even fresher smile. She's wearing loose pants, a crisp white shirt, and buckled boots. You never see women wear pants, or a sword. Yet she's added a second cutlass to her belt. She released her sleek hair to feel the freedom of the wind. She must have found the captain's closet because she's wearing Rodriguez's hat too.

She swaggers over to us, picks the rum out of our hands, and tosses it overboard.

"Hey! We were just celebrating!" Charlie shouts.

"You need to be alert! How long before we intercept the *Endurance*?"

"I dunno. I'll have to check the charts." Charlie reaches for another bottle of rum, but Isabelle slaps his hand.

"You haven't done that already? So, you mean to tell me that we aren't on course? At this rate, we could miss the *Endurance* and her gold entirely. And just why are we flying the black?" She points to Rodriguez's flag flapping above us—a white skull and Catholic cross embossed above two white pistols. "Real pirates don't gallivant around flying the black. They fly friendly colors and then raise the black right before they take a ship."

She turns to me. I accidentally stagger back. She's fierce. "Is this how you plan to command your new ship, Captain James? Sloppy. We need a course and we need to anticipate Captain Rodriguez's retribution. How long do you think it'll take him to get a new ship? Not long by my reckoning. We've risked everything and you two are up here dulling your senses and laughing at the ocean." She picks up the crate of rum and tosses it over the railing.

Charlie reaches to stop her, but the rum is already sinking into the sea.

His mouth hangs open. Isabelle isn't the sort of girl he's used to. She's a little more... fiery. But he quickly comes to his senses. "That bay we left Rodriguez in was two days, by ship, from the nearest port. It'll take him weeks to procure a new ship if he even manages to reach civilization."

Rodriguez will find his way to a port. Even if he has to string his crew together as a raft. Charlie hadn't seen the devil in Rodriguez's eyes. Isabelle had a point. Rodriguez would find a new ship and we would be his first target.

Rodriguez never forgets. He only forgives after penance.

Isabelle swings her head toward me and starts making demands. "We need a heading. Are you going to do something about that, James, or am I going to have to start a mutiny for anything to get done around here?"

I imagine she used this tone for ordering people around in the governor's mansion. Part of me rears back at Isabelle's bossiness, but the rest of me admires it. She could have been a pirate captain. She could've been anything.

"My God, Isabelle," Charlie finally stutters.

I decide to concede to her demands, build a little trust, build a little friendship. "Fine, fine. Let's head down to the captain's cabin and we'll make a plan."

"That's better." She struts over to me, smiles, and takes the captain's hat off her head and puts it on mine.

I'm not exactly sure what to make of the gesture, but I liked it. It felt playful. I adjust the hat and tip it to her.

"Humpf." She sizes me up, trying to discern if I can deliver the wealth I promised. She looks through my eyes to see what lies behind. *What sort of person are you, James?* She must have liked what she found in my soul. She doesn't scowl before taking her leave. "And Charlie, take down the black! Fly English colors tonight. For all you know we could bump into the *London Wolf.*"

Charlie looks at me, rubs his eyes, and shakes his head. "What a woman."

"Yeah. She's right about Rodriguez's flag. We had best take it down."

"*Take down the black, Charlie.*" He mumbles as he pulls the rope to lower the flag. He raises the crisscrossing blue and red lines of the British. "*Fly English colors, Charlie. You never know when you might bump into Captain Solway.*"

———

"Ahoy there!" A voice calls out through the dark. "This is Captain Solway of the *London Wolf.* Identify yourself."

A patrolling English warship sails alongside us. Two rows of cannon hatches protrude above the waterline. All of them are pointed toward us. The *London Wolf* is a Goliath that makes the *San Paulo* look like David. She sits ten feet higher in the water than us, so I can't see the crew aboard, but I can imagine. Probably at least two hundred men. Thank God we got the English flag up when we did.

"Ahoy! What is the name of this vessel and your destination?" Captain Solway, the famous pirate hunter, calls again. He looks down from the railing of his ship. Even while at sea, he wears his full uniform—a heavy red coat, white powdered wig, and tall Naval officer's hat. His face is long and comes to a sharp point toward the end of his nose. Like an arrow tip pointed at his prey. "Identify yourself or we'll be forced to come aboard."

"We're the—the *Goat's Horn*." Charlie steps in front of the crumpled pirate flag, hoping to hide it from Solway's view.

"What kind of stupid name is the *Goat's Horn*?" I whisper.

"The *Goat's Horn*?" Captain Solway scowls. "What is your destination and cargo?"

"Uh, goats." Charlie covers his mouth and goes *"meh"* like a goat bleating from below deck. "And we're headed for… St. Augustine."

"You're headed where? I didn't catch that last bit," Captain Solway says.

"St. Augustine is a Spanish port. The British hate the Spanish," I whisper.

"We're headed for Barbados," Charlie corrects.

Captain Solway raises an eyebrow. "You're certainly taking the long way."

"This route is safer. With the great Captain Solway patrolling the waters and all…" Charlie says.

"Ah, very well. But be careful. We have reports of the *San Paulo* being sighted in these waters. You haven't seen them, have you?"

Charlie shakes his head. "No, of course not. Just been quiet sailing tonight."

"Be safe then, and goodnight."

The *London Wolf* lumbers off. As she leaves I see the wake of her stern. It's hard to believe such a massive object can still move.

Charlie sits down and leans against the railing of the ship. "Comforting to know that monster of a ship is just lurking about, isn't it?"

NATHAN SMITH

I slump down next to him and release a deep breath. "We'll need to be more watchful."

"Hey, James." He motions me to come close and then checks over his shoulder. "I've been thinking. Captain Rodriguez was going to ransom Isabelle back to her father in Havana. We could too. Once we relieve the *Endurance* of her gold, we could drop Isabelle off in Havana or some other Spanish port before setting sail for Africa. Imagine, the gold from the *Endurance* plus her ransom. And there'd only be two shares then."

"I thought you liked Isabelle," I say.

He smiles a greedy grin. "I do, but I like treasure more."

I chuckle. "You've turned into a proper pirate. All right, you and me." I shake his hand.

Isabelle is delightful, truly, but ransoming her off would mean that much more gold for me and Charlie.

When it comes to treasure, a lot is never enough. I've been in the company of pirates long enough to know. The only amount that will ever be enough is every penny you can squeeze from the world.

Now it's time to squeeze.

We head below deck to plan our course and our encounter with the *Endurance*.

4

THE PLAN

Rodriguez was a collector of oddities. Mayan talismans, native spears, colorful shields, even a pair of elephant's tusks are set out about the captain's cabin. Isabelle has already lit lamps and is waiting for us. She's reclined in the old captain's chair, her feet propped on a tobacco barrel, reading a book from the shelf. Rodriguez was illiterate, but he liked books.

She looks up from her copy of *Julius Caesar* and says, "What took you two so long?"

"Charlie couldn't hold his rum and needed someone to hold back his hair," I lie to obscure that we were plotting her betrayal.

Charlie gives me a mean look for embarrassing him in front of Isabelle.

"That's best. Maybe it'll teach you two a lesson. That stuff will kill you. I had an uncle drink himself to death. Anyway, down to business."

She sets down her book, stands, and then unrolls a sea map. It crackles to its full length across the antique desk. The old wood is pocketed with bullet holes and sword cut groves. The desk looks to have seen as much combat as Rodriguez.

Isabelle motions for me to look at the map. I've studied many things, but I never learned the subtle art of navigation. That was probably short sighted.

"Charlie, you're our navigator. Do your thing," I say.

He squints at me, still chaffed over the puke comment. He runs his fingers across the map of crisscrossing latitude and longitude lines, islands, sea monsters, wrecks, and the location of the *Endurance*.

Charlie takes a quill from the ink well and draws a line across the map. We'll only need this map once. "Alright, this is the *Endurance*'s course."

The line cuts through the stretch of ocean between the Florida Keys and the Northern tip of Cuba. "This arpeggio here creates a natural wall. This is where we need to intercept the *Endurance*. She'll have no place to run and this is a remote stretch of ocean. Few other ships pass this way, except the *London Wolf*, apparently. But nothing we can do about that."

"If few ships take this route, why is the *Endurance* going this way?" Isabelle asks.

"Because few other ships pass this way," Charlie says.

"Anonymity." I guess our opposing captain's intentions. "The *Endurance* is a massive treasure ship. She wants to avoid the heavily pirated waters."

Isabelle laughs. "Her captain will be in a for surprise then."

That he will be. The decision the *Endurance*'s captain made was a gamble. He avoids the heavily pirated sea routes but leaves himself isolated. He rolled the dice, but I got the winning numbers.

"Where are we now?" I ask.

Charlie locates the remote bay where the *San Paulo* was anchored before we stole it. "We were here. We've been headed North for about three hours. I'll have to go above deck and check the star charts to get our exact location, but we're about here." He points to a patch of open ocean.

"I'll check our exact location and then adjust our course so that we reach the intercept before the *Endurance*. We'll lay in hiding behind the arpeggio and spring out when they're near." He walks a needle point compass across the map to measure the distance to our destination. "We should be there by tomorrow afternoon, right on schedule with Rodriguez's plan."

24

Isabelle taps her knuckles to the desk. "Good, that'll give us time to plan for our encounter. What's the plan, James?"

When we stole the *San Paulo*, we also commandeered Rodriguez's plan to rob the *Endurance*. Rodriguez must have spent weeks tracking the *Endurance*. He frittered hundreds of English Pounds to loosen the tongues of British sailors. He had probably been planning to rob the *Endurance* for months, but it took mere hours for us to seize the plan.

Sure, there's only three of us. The plan will play differently than Rodriguez imagined, but the original idea is intact. "We show up and they surrender, like every other ship in the past eight months."

"But what happens if they don't surrender?" Isabelle asks. "This is the largest shipment of gold out of the New World in years. They might want to defend that."

They can't put up a fight. Because if they do, my clever plan will go down in a blaze of British cannon fire, be sliced to pieces by British cutlasses, and rot forever in a godforsaken British prison cell.

"We'll need a back-up plan," Isabelle says, "and I think I've got one. I've been below deck, inspecting the cannons. I think I can rig a rope and pulley system to open all the cannon hatch doors at once. Then, if necessary, I can run down the row and light them all. We'll preload the cannons tomorrow. This won't do us much good in a real battle—there's only three of us—but it could give us enough diversion to escape or intimidate."

Charlie looks up from the map toward Isabelle. "You enjoy this, don't you?"

"The pirate's life is the life for me. Yo-ho."

Despite the sarcasm, she can't hide that she finds pleasure in the intricacies of our plan. I'm surprised she didn't think to steal the ship before I did. She has a tactician's mind. A carefully trained muscle she never had the chance to flex in real competition. Until tonight, that is.

"Isabelle's right. Having it rigged that way will be useful," I say.

"And it will give the illusion that the ship is fully manned. If the *Endurance* begins to think, if even for a second, that it's just the three of us on board, they'll overrun us. We'll have to trick them." Isabelle spins a pistol across the map.

"How? Scarecrows?" Charlie asks.

"No, you dunce. We'll position rifles along the railing of the boat so that it looks like our 'crew' is taking cover, prepared for a fight. Our ship sits high in the water. Our deck is higher than theirs. That means their crew won't be able to see our numbers, but their lookout can. We'll have to take him out."

"How do you know our deck is higher than the *Endurance*'s?" I ask.

"I've see the *Endurance*, many times. She often makes port in Havana, in secret of course. They might not be at war anymore, but Spain and Great Britain aren't friends. My father makes an exception for the *Endurance*'s captain. They're old compadres."

"So, you know the captain?" I ask.

The captain sounds eerily familiar. I'm praying it's not who I think it is. I too once knew a Brit with a special friendship with Havana's governor.

And the governor—I've known him since I was a boy. Formal dress was never to his taste, so he wore commoner's clothes—a loose white shirt and trousers. His hair was a thick salt and pepper when I knew him, but his eyes were lively.

You don't forget meeting a man like Francisco Cardoso, governor of Havana. The fire Isabelle carries must've been passed down from him. He's a Spanish idealist at odds with the Spanish crown. "Too forward thinking" is how the king describes him. Yet the king can't argue with the gold mine Governor Cardoso shaped Havana into. For that the king endures his eccentricities.

"I've met the captain of the *Endurance*," Isabelle says. "He's a cold and a calculating man. Honorable though. He'll be difficult to fool. It honestly wouldn't surprise me if he tried to fight even if he thought we were fully manned. He's not a man to be trifled with. His name is Admiral William Higgins."

My heart stops. No. William Higgins is—

Charlie stands up. "You couldn't have mentioned that we'd be facing the toughest Admiral in the British navy before we took the ship of the most notorious pirate in the world? You didn't think to tell us how deep the privy was before we jumped in looking for treasure?"

William Higgins has a strong reputation. In addition to his military honors, he was once a famous pirate hunter, but gave that up sixteen years ago, after he had a son.

I snap back to reality. "It wouldn't have made a difference. We would have still stolen this ship. I've not known either of you long, but I know you well enough to know you don't shy away from danger when there's treasure involved. Admiral Higgins will break down." It feels odd calling the man *Admiral.* "All men break when they see Captain Rodriguez's flag."

I hope the Admiral will surrender. His decision to fight or surrender is hard to predict. I could see it going either way—a flip of the coin.

"That brings us to our next problem," Isabelle says. "We'll need a Rodriguez."

"And just where are we going to get another Rodriguez?" Charlie asks. "Are we going to stop by a merchant's shop and pick one up on the way? Why do we need him anyway? We've got his flag and his ship."

"Men aren't afraid of Rodriguez's flag or of his ship, they're afraid of Rodriguez."

Charlie pauses and thinks for a moment. "We'll tell them the captain's sick and below deck."

"Yes, because that will strike fear into their hearts."

"Well, let's dress James up as captain. What are the chances that the crew of the *Endurance* has actually seen Captain Rodriguez in real life? We could dress the goat as Rodriguez for how well these men know him."

Isabelle shakes her head. "No offense, but James is too dark and you're too skinny. They'll never buy it."

"Then where do you expect us to find a perfect copy of Captain Rodriguez?"

"Calm down, we'll figure that part out later." I rub my eyes. I'm getting tired. It's been an eventful day.

"We've got another even more pressing problem," Isabelle says.

"You're such a raincloud. Can we just deal with it in the morning?" Charlie rummages through Captain Rodriguez's desk for another bottle of rum.

"Deal with it in the morning? We'll be up all night making the necessary arrangements for our intercept. And no, I'm not a raincloud. I'm a realist. You're both lucky I'm here or you would've run head-first into this and gotten yourselves killed. We need to figure out how they'll deliver the treasure. They can't bring it on deck. They would see there's only three of us. And we can't board their ship because they'll realize how young we are."

I slap my forehead. She's right. How could I not have thought of all this? I look at the map. We need a viable way to transfer the treasure from their ship to the *San Paulo*.

"Well, what do you suggest, princess?" Charlie is getting agitated.

"Governors daughters are not princesses. And I don't know, but we'll have to come up with something."

"All problems and no plans, you are. Isn't it bad luck to have a woman on board a ship or something like that?"

"I've brought you considerable luck! Without me, you would've both been dead by now."

"We could've handled ourselves, right James? James?"

I'm not listening. I'm too busy scouring the map, intimidating it into giving me its secrets.

Perhaps their ship would have a loading crane—some ships do—but even then, they would have to come too close. So that's no good. They could bring the treasure over on jolly boats, but then those men would come aboard to see an empty ship. Besides, I don't think Charlie and I could lift all of the treasure. I eye the map, but there's nothing near the intercept location except the arpeggio of islands.

The islands!

Charlie and Isabelle are still bickering, tossing insults back and forth. Isabelle rears her fist back to knock out Charlie's teeth and—

"I've got it!" I say.

They look at me.

I point at the map. "We'll make them leave the treasure on one of these islands and tell them to leave. Then we collect it at our leisure when they're gone."

Isabelle frowns. "They'll find that suspicious. That isn't how pirates operate. Now that I think about it, I've never heard of stolen cargo being transferred like that."

"Captain Rodriguez has always been eccentric. He changes the rules all the time. They'll just think its him being his usual odd self."

"Maybe. It's hard to say. We still need to find ourselves a 'Captain Rodriguez' though—"

A man staggers in through the cabin door, brandishing a stool in one hand and a floppy fish in the other. His hair is matted with blood and he's got a crazed look in his eyes.

"Who in the blazes is this?" Charlie asks.

But I recognize him instantly. We forgot about the pirate we left tied up in the brig.

We didn't throw him overboard. He must have wiggled free. Now he's ready to single handily take back the ship. He lurches into the cabin and regains his footing. He's still a little drunk, and obviously not up to a fight. "What're you kids doing with Captain Rodriguez's ship?"

"Our ship now," I say.

Time to be captain and give commands.

"Charlie," I say. Charlie looks up from the map and awaits my instructions. "Get him."

5

THE SURROGATE

"I think he's waking up," Charlie says. The pirate's head wobbles with the sway of the boat. His mouth hangs open, but he is certainly not waking up. We've got him tied to a chair in the captain's cabin for now. Poor guy has had a rough go at it. Even before we got a hold of him, it seems. His face is wrinkled, and his stubble beard is uneven. One of his eyes is larger than the other and is as yellow as his teeth.

"He's just gurgling or dying or something like that. I told you to tie him up, not beat him over the head with an oar!" I say.

"No, you distinctly said, 'get him' and I said I was sorry!"

I poke the pirate with the handle of my dagger. "What are we going to do with him?"

And just what else have we forgotten? Did we leave the cannons behind? Is Rodriguez himself stowed in the galley? I know my plan is crazy and shouldn't have even gotten us this far, but who would've thought commandeering a pirate ship would be so perilous?

"Splash some water in his face," Isabelle says.

Charlie looks around. "All we've got in here is rum."

"That'll do."

"But…"

"We're certainly not going to run out of it. Not aboard this ship. Just do it."

Charlie splashes rum in the old pirate's face and he sputters back to life, eyes wide with fear and confusion. "Hail Mary, mother of God…"

"So, what do we do with him?" I ask.

"Throw him over like we did the others I suppose. I've always wanted to make someone walk the plank." Charlie grins.

The pirate's eyes widen.

"Throwing him over in the middle of sea is tantamount to killing him," Isabelle says.

"And I can't swim," the old pirate says, looking to Isabelle as a friend. She's not as inclined as Charlie to throw him overboard.

"What kind of pirate can't swim?" Charlie asks.

"This one."

"We'll maroon him on the next island we pass," I say.

"Yes, that'll do." Charlie rubs his hands together.

Isabelle strokes her chin like she's thinking. "You're both missing it. This is the solution to our problem. Just look at him."

She steps over to the old pirate, brushes tattered hair out of his face, and lifts his chin. She tilts his face from side to side, examining his features in the dim light. She nods her head and smiles. "He'll be our Captain Rodriguez."

"Him? He's a drunk!" Charlie says.

"I'm inclined to agree with Charlie. He looks nothing like Captain Rodriguez."

"I can fix that." Isabelle appraises the old pirate once more. "I spent years learning how to apply men's and women's makeup. I know how to make people look younger and more beautiful than they actually are. It's just another art of deception and I'm a master of it. You won't even recognize him when I'm done."

"Isn't he a little fat to be Rodriguez?" Charlie pokes the old man's belly.

"I've got a corset in the luggage Rodriguez stole when he kidnapped me."

"We don't even know if we can trust him," I say.

"Oh, you can trust me, all right. I'm the honorable sort." The old pirate nods his head hopefully.

"The honorable sort who is willing to take advantage of young, imprisoned girls?" Isabelle asks.

He blushes and ducks his head. "Never said I was perfect."

Isabelle looks at me. I shrug my shoulders. Might as well give this a shot. Without this man we'd be limited to painting my face white. Or stuffing Charlie's clothes with hay and standing him on a box. It's not like a surrogate for Captain Rodriguez is going to fall from the sky or be fished from the ocean. He's a little old, a little fat, and very shifty, but we have to work with what we've got.

"What's your name and position aboard this ship?" I ask.

"Gunther Winkworth, cook aboard the *San Paulo*. At your service, Captain…" He bows his head and awaits my name.

"Captain James. Will you serve under me?"

"Aye, sir."

"How do I know you won't betray me?"

"I'm the cook, sir. The cook is loyal to whoever happens to be the current captain, or whoever pays his salary…" Gunther smiles.

I look at Charlie and Isabelle. Charlie looks unsure, but Isabelle gives an approving nod.

Gunther'll do.

"And if you need more proof than that, remember I wasn't exactly one of the captain's favorites. He left me aboard the ship the night of the celebration and all—"

"That'll do, Gunther. Untie him," I say.

"But, Captain." Charlie looks concerned.

I take out my lucky doubloon and hold it up in the dim light. "Heads we trust him, tails we throw him overboard. Is that fair, Charlie?"

"Alright."

Gunther struggles in his bindings, unhappy his fate is being determined by the flip on a coin. "Now, just hold up there, Captain—"

I flick the coin into the air. Gunther gasps, Charlie smiles, and I catch the coin and slap it to my wrist. Theatrically, I lift my hand to reveal the Spanish king's face. Heads.

Gunther lets out a long sigh. "You three are mad. All of you, crazy as cats with bells tied to their tails."

"Cut him loose, Charlie."

Charlie grumbles as he takes out his knife. "All I wanted to go do was maroon someone or at the very least make them walk the plank. I imagine making someone walk the plank is a rite of passage among buccaneers. But no. Let's befriend the cutthroat pirate."

Charlie cuts the rope and Gunter feels his neck and wrists where the rope had been tied.

"Might as well tell him the plan, James," Isabelle says.

"We're going to steal the treasure from the *Endurance*."

Gunther laughs so hard at the notion that he nearly chokes on it. He wipes a tear from his eye and stutters, "The three of you? Or do you plan to pick up a few other ruffians in Tortuga first?" before he breaks down in maniacal laughter.

"The four of us," Isabelle says, reminding him that he is now as much a part of this plan as we are.

"You really plan to do this?" Gunther sighs, lowers his head, grumbles a bit, and then says, "You're serious, aren't you? Just how do you plan to relieve a warship of her gold?"

I pull a chair up in front of Gunther and sit to where my eyes meet his. I learned this tactic from watching my father. It gives the impression that you and the person you're speaking to are equals. The reality is you're lowering yourself to their level. And they know it. They know you're truly higher than them. My father is a brilliant tactician. I may not like him, but our adversaries are often our greatest teachers.

"We're relying on the feared reputation of Captain Rodriguez. Ships no longer try to fight him. If we're sailing his ship and flying his flag, the *Endurance* will surrender."

"That's a bold plan, Master James. You must have balls of a—" He glances at Isabelle and checks his language.

Isabelle spouts a string of curses that make Gunther, a lifelong pirate, blush. She knows her way around inappropriate language. That must've caused a stir in the governor's mansion.

"I suppose I can speak freely in your presence?"

"Aye."

"Are you three sure they'll surrender?" he asks.

"I believe they will," I say.

Gunther is silent for a moment, obviously turning thoughts in his mind, trying to decide which of them to let out.

"There's something the three of you should know. This gem is free, but my other services will cost you. Many of the crew were skeptical about the *Endurance*. They were content to deliver Miss Cardoso here for ransom and be done. They worried the *Endurance*'s crew would put up too much of a fight, so the captain came to address us.

"He said, and I quote, 'Those tea sipping, lobster-backs have a treasure bigger than your mother's bosom and you're going to let the king take it? You've gotten lazy with all the ships surrendering lately. Sure, the *Endurance* will probably put up a fight, but do we or do we not have our ship armed to the teeth? If you boys don't follow me into this, I'll sail the *San Paulo* up to the Fortress of Long Rock and fire off a cannon while you're sleeping. I'll teach you lot how to fight again, or I'll get myself a new crew who aren't so dainty.'"

"Captain Rodriguez expected resistance from the *Endurance*?" Isabelle asks.

"It's hard to say with the captain. Sometimes he would give us the exact same speech before we took a grain ship. Probably nothing. Shouldn't have mentioned it. Don't want to spook my three newest little friends." Gunther smiles and shrugs. "Rodriguez did odd things."

Isabelle and Charlie look at me. Conflicting forces wage war within them. Their greed is wrestling with their common sense, each trying to choke the other into submission.

If even Rodriguez was expecting a fight...

My greed too wrestles with my fear. But I kill them both. There is only treasure; there are only men who are strong enough to take it. Or men so weak as to let treasure pass without it realizing it had been in the sights of pirates.

As if he can sense the growing doubt in each of us, Gunther breaks the silence. "How do the three of you plan to maneuver this ship into position to intercept with the Endurance? It takes at least six men on the mast to manage the wind, and another at the helm. How will the three of you manage that?"

Isabelle coughs. "The four of us."

"Aye. The four of us. Four still doesn't make seven."

Some things you can control, some things you can't. Half our lives are controlled by fate; the other half is controlled by our reaction to fate. Control what you can, anticipate what you can't. We can't control what the *Endurance* does, but we can make our preparations. We can figure out how to make all the cannon doors open at once, and how to sail the ship with only four crewmen.

"We're working on it," I say.

"I can help rig a good system for you," Gunther says.

"That would be appreciated."

Gunther looks down, making calculations in his mind. "I'll be expecting a share of the treasure."

"A share? We didn't throw you overboard! That's your share," Charlie says.

Men who work deserve their pay. I can afford to pay Gunther, if he fulfills his end of the bargain.

"Do you know how much treasure is aboard the *Endurance*, Charlie?" I say. "More than enough to offer this man a fair share for his services."

Gunther smiles a grimy smile lacking several teeth.

Now to seal the new alliance. "You will play the role of Captain Rodriguez. And before the intercept, you will work with Charlie to rig a way to steer the ship during our encounter. You two will have to come up with something clever. Are you in for this?"

I offer my hand. Best to seal this sort of thing with a firm handshake.

Gunther stands up. He accepts my handshake but grabs my forearm —the way wild men of the sea do. He looks me in the eye and says, "I've always wanted to be a pirate captain, but this plan is a heap of dung that's going to splatter in your faces. It'll never work, but I'm old. Better to die with your boots on I suppose. I'm in."

I take back what I said about men who work deserving their pay and about honoring bargains. If we find a better Captain Rodriguez surrogate on the way, I'm throwing this man overboard.

"It'll work," Isabelle says.

"If this works, and three kids steal the treasure of the *Endurance*, I'll eat my hat."

"I see another problem," Charlie says. "Captain Rodriguez had a long beard. Unless Gunther here can make his grow by three inches overnight, we'll have a problem."

Isabelle laughs. "Don't worry, I saw a goat in the cargo hold. He'll happily provide a nice beard."

A corset, a goat hair beard, beauty treatments. Gunther groans, probably wishing we'd have just thrown him over and been done with it before we made off with the *San Paulo*.

6

FATE

Cool air greets me as I climb from the underbelly of the ship. The *San Paulo* glides through the night, making fair speed as the calm sea splashes against the hull. The moon completes itself where the ocean meets the sky, half of it real, the other half a reflection in the water. A clear sky and bright stars shine on my newfound captaincy.

I've come above deck to inspect Charlie and Gunther's work on the rigging. I suppose this is the sort of thing a captain does. Gunther made a good point; the sails would need to be cleverly managed.

Before coming above deck, I made a quick stop in the captain's closet. A new captain should look the part. Rodriguez was taller than me. Other than his pant legs being a little too long, his clothes fit me fine. I don't know what Isabelle was talking about—I could've played the part of Captain Rodriguez. Well, could've if my skin was a few shades lighter.

I kept the hat Isabelle gave me, obviously. I found some new brown trousers, a loose shirt, a thick belt with two pistol holsters that I slung over my shoulder. I fastened a thinner one around my waist. I buckled a shiny pair of boots that click as I walk the deck, inspecting my crew's work.

Ropes hang like a mess of vines among jungle trees. Only the main mast is cloaked with sail. The other two masts are reefed. Pulleys, ropes, hammers, and other sail parts are littered about the deck.

I breathe deep the night air. I need it after the time spent cooped up in the captain's cabin developing devious plans. We'll work through the night to prepare for our intercept with the *Endurance*.

Charlie is up the center mast and Gunther is at the base, yelling, "Get those riggings tight, Master Charlie! If they fail, we'll be dead in the water after we finish with the *Endurance*. That'll look odd. They'll be curious. They might come check on us. We have to make it appear that things aboard this ship are operating normally."

"If you're so concerned about this, then why don't you get your fat self up here and do it yourself?"

"You'd make an old man climb up there?"

Charlie grumbles to the night wind and 'accidentally' drops a pulley. Gunther hobbles out of the way before it slams against the deck.

I step from the shadows and say, "What've you two geniuses managed to concoct?"

He startles, on edge from having his head beaten with a rum bottle, thrashed by an oar, and nearly crushed by a pulley. "It's actually quite clever. Charlie learned more about ship-craft from the old captain than he lets on. He's a brilliant lad at this sort of thing. Has a good mind for ropes, maps, and sails. I'll wait for him to come down, so he can explain this contraption."

"Is he almost finished?"

"I dunno, let me see. You about done yet, Master Charlie?"

"Would you give me a minute, you lard?"

"He'll be done in a minute."

"I assume we're on course," I say.

"Aye, Captain. Charlie set us in the right direction before climbing up to fix the mast. Good clear night for sailing, easy to find our position from the stars. Charlie did that too. I learned a little about navigation in my early years, but Charlie didn't need no help."

I nod approvingly and lean against the railing to wait.

Gunther leans next to me. He lays his arms on the railing and writhes his hands over the churning sea. "I'll tell you straight. I don't particularly like you and your lot. Don't trust you. The three of you have devil's minds. It's unnatural. You're all too smart for your age—too cunning. And you're far too quick to upset the status quo. Don't expect me to follow you around being your Captain Rodriguez after this whole thing is over." He looks me in the eye to let me know this part of the deal is non-negotiable.

It's obvious that he's spent a lifetime among dangerous men. He has no intention of wrapping himself up in a tangled alliance. He may be fat and damaged in the head, but more than that, he is worn. I think he wants to take his treasure and find some place quiet. Somewhere there's no English or Spanish, no pirates, and no little schemers like me, Charlie, and Isabelle.

"We'll be done with the pirate life after this. This sort of plan can only work once. Once Rodriguez makes it back to port, word will spread that he's no longer aboard the *San Paulo*. Without the captain, the flag is a weak banner, limp in the wind, and the ship may as well be a dingy. As for me and my lot, we'll be headed somewhere remote to hide after this. We'll drop you off somewhere along the way."

Charlie and I will be, at least. Isabelle will be ransomed back to her father.

"That'll be best. You three are smart, you could be great pirates, greater than Rodriguez or Black Beard or Vane. Rodriguez and Marcello are the last two big names out there. The rest are dead. Didn't know when to stop. Don't go getting a hunger for treasure, James. Be content when you've got enough. That's the wisest thing to do. Or one day, you'll reach too far. One more spoil isn't worth risking your whole legacy. You could be infamous, or you could sit happily on a beach somewhere."

Maybe Gunther is a bit wiser than I realized. Insightful if nothing else. The fact that he spent a lifetime as a pirate should say something. You don't see many old pirates.

We're quiet for a moment while I contemplate his words. Charlie and I will stop with the treasure of the *Endurance*. No need for anything more after that.

No, wait, we'll stop after Isabelle's ransom.

Or is that over reaching, like Gunther spoke of? Should we stop when we gain the ultimate prize? Would Isabelle's ransom be so grand?

I'm alone with my thoughts until Gunther speaks. "Where'll you be headed?"

"I'd prefer not to say."

"Still don't trust me, eh?"

Charlie swings like a monkey from the upper rigging. He lands feet first on the deck of the ship. "One more mast to go, but I'll finish after I explain how this works."

"What's the plan?" I ask.

"The ship has three masts. On our approach to the *Endurance*, we will have the main mast open. It will be enough to carry us to their position. To stop, we'll set the sail loose and let it fly off with the wind. I've got a rope strung to the bridge that will drop the sail once pulled. After the sail has dropped, we'll lose the wind and slow down to a stop. We'll have to carefully judge when to drop it, seeing as we no longer have an anchor to slow us down. We'll coast up to the *Endurance*."

I'm not the most seasoned sailor, but that's not how it's normally done. "Won't that look a little odd?"

"Yes, but it's the best I can manage. Hopefully, they'll just chalk it up to Captain Rodriguez's eccentricity. Most times, there'd be men up there to reef the sail, but we don't have enough manpower to do that. We'll need to come to a stop to intercept the *Endurance*."

"And then to get us moving again, once they've delivered the treasure to the island?"

"We will use the front mast, which I just strung. Normally, there'd be men up there to let it loose, but I've figured out a better way. I've run a rope with pulleys over to the bridge. I've rigged the sail so that when you pull the rope, it drops."

Gunther nudges me with his elbow. "Told you it was quite a brilliant system."

"What's the mast at the stern to be used for?" I ask.

"I'll be rigging it the same as the front mast, to be dropped from a rope at the bridge. It'll be used if…if we need to make a quick getaway," Charlie says.

"I see. Hopefully we won't need it." In the back of my mind, I'm thankful that Charlie had this foresight. I would never tell my crew this, but I'm worried about our interception with the *Endurance*.

My father is Admiral William Higgins, Captain of our prize, the *Endurance*. This may complicate things. My mother was a slave in Charleston who I've never met. After I was born, my father fled Charleston and kept me in his house in Barbados. I was the only black mark in his whole career, but yet he refused to disown me, regardless of all the slander.

I knew he was in the navy, but it's been nearly three years since I last saw him. I didn't know he had been promoted to Admiral. I had no idea where or what ship he was stationed on. When I ran away, I never wanted to see him again, but it seems fate put him on the *Endurance*.

Fate is a set dice. Sometimes the lot is cast in your favor, sometimes it isn't. Yet more often than it should, fate carries you to moments of redemption or retribution. It puts you in a place to make critical choices at the junctions of your life. It carries you back to people you left on the other side of the world and makes you question whether you have control over your own life or someone in the sky is pulling the puppet strings.

I suppose I'm now fated to see my father once more. Just because I see him doesn't mean he'll have to see me. I'll keep my head down in the encounter, stay out of his sight. If I play it right, he'll never know his son was only a gangplank away.

My father has a special relationship with the Governor of Havana. Spain and England may be enemies, but the friendship between he and my father goes further back than the war that recently ended. They've been friends since they were children. That's why my father is secretly allowed to make port in Havana's harbor—flying a Spanish flag of course.

Their relationship was always a bit odd from what I saw. As I mentioned before, Governor Francisco Cardoso is an idealist. He never spoke to me much, but he looked at me differently than others. He looked at me like my father did—like I was a person with a soul, not an object to be owned. I liked the Governor. He and my father were best friends. They were also schemers. But I never knew what they were scheming.

I never sat in on their meetings. My father made me wait outside when the governor secretly came to visit him in Barbados under the cover of night.

The navy forced my father away from home often, but the frequent meetings with the Governor in both Havana and Barbados ate into the little spare time he had. Because of this, even when he was home, he wasn't. His mind was always elsewhere, focused on the schemes he and the governor were drawing.

I grew to resent him for it. Why keep me if he had no time for me? It would be better for both of us if I was gone. He'd no longer have his black mark. I'd no longer be forced to be loved at such a distance that I never felt love's warm embrace.

My father's relationship with the governor might be useful though. There might be a way to ransom Isabelle to my father during the encounter and let him deliver her back to the Governor. I'll have to speak to Charlie about the details.

I haven't told my crew that Admiral William Higgins is my father. No need to worry them, but I know my father. He's smart and honorable—a gentleman who stands clean and tall. I don't know if it's true, but he told me he tried to marry my mother. While the Crown would tolerate him keeping a mixed bastard, they would not stand for an interracial marriage.

For him the choice of honor when the *San Paulo* threatens his cargo will be this: sparing the lives of his men from Captain Rodriguez de Medina, or honor in defending the king's treasure. It will be a hard choice for my father.

Our act will have to be flawless. We can leave no room in my father to doubt. He must think this ship is fully armed.

My thoughts return to the *San Paulo's* preparations and to the glances of Charlie and Gunther.

"Captain?" Gunther says.

I was lost in thought and had left the conversation behind.

"Keep up the good work, gentlemen," I say, quickly. "Finish the final mast. Gunther, when you're finished, prepare some dinner. And Charlie, when you're done, join me below deck to help Isabelle complete the preparations on our cannons."

I turn to leave. I take one more gulp of the fresh air before being confined below deck to make the necessary modifications. When we're done with her, the *San Paulo* will be a horrid abomination of a pirate ship.

She'll beg us to scuttle her.

7

A DRAGON IN YOUR HAND

CAPTAIN RODRIGUEZ WAS PARANOID AND TENDED TO BE OVER zealous. This dangerous combination explains why the *San Paulo*, a ship only meant to carry twenty cannons, is laden with—I quickly take count —nearly forty, stuffed into rows like carefully nurtured crops.

The same can also be said for the ordinance the ship carries. Barrels of gunpowder and neat pyramids of cannon balls clutter the room. The crew maintained pathways. The captain stuffed more ammunition down here every time the ship made port. He'd be damned if he got into a fight and lost because he ran out of firepower.

The ceilings are low, the air is thick, and glass lamps hang from the ceiling to give Isabelle light to work by. In the dim light, she wipes sweat from her brow. She reaches toward the pulley she hammered above the cannon hatch.

For a cannon to fire, the hatches must open. Usually, the cannons would be pulled forward, so the tip would stick out the breech. We won't be able to do that. They'll have to fire from where they sit. That leaves a slight risk that, if their aim is off, the cannons could blow a hole in the side of the ship. It's unlikely and the hole would be far above the waterline.

But anyone watching a cannon blow a hole in its own ship would find that fishy. Ships don't just blow holes in themselves. Any opposing captain worth his salt would know that something was amiss. Like that the cannons were improperly fired was because there weren't enough crew to man them. Or that the ship was being sailed by three misfits.

But what is far more likely to blow a hole in the ship, and far more pressing, is the fire from one of Isabelle's lamps. If one of those hits the floor, it'll blow the ship across the Atlantic and back to Europe.

"Should you have those lamps lit down here? You know, with all this gunpowder? Maybe we should do this in the morning." I blow out a few of the extra lamps.

I've always been intimidated by gunpowder. You can hold it in your hand, keep it in barrels, you can store it, but you can't control it. You can only control what it comes in contact with. A little flame and boom. It's like people, reactive, quick to change, quick to go from stable to an explosion.

I've never trusted gunpowder.

Or people.

"Are you an expert on these things now, Captain James? It'll be fine. They're glass bottled lamps. But if you hear me mutter a curse word, you might want to run." She brushes her hair out of her face and laughs. "Or if you see me jump out this hatch into the ocean, you might want to do the same."

"Thanks for the advanced warning. What've you rigged up?"

"I'll show you in a second. I'm almost done. Come hold the lamp for me while I tie off this last door."

Ropes and pulleys are strung like a spider web between hammocks and cannons. Some are taut, others are loose. Like a jungle for us to prowl.

She has cooked up something clever.

Maybe Gunther was right, perhaps we do have devil's minds. Charlie is simply smart in his own right. He has a way of understanding complex systems like rigging and navigation. It comes naturally to him. Isabelle is educated, but also has an inborn intelligence. I'm educated, but none of it came easy. I had to cleave the knowledge from books.

My education was the source of my plan to steal the *San Paulo*. No way could I have concocted a plan like this if I hadn't read about a handful of Spartans taking Troy, or Odysseus killing the cyclops with only a few men. To uneducated men like Gunther, knowledge and other ideas beaten from the spines of books look like witchcraft.

But it's not witchcraft. It's mostly repetition. My father was my teacher. He taught me arithmetic, history, to read, and to write. We sat in the parlor of our home and he helped me form my letters. He would hold his hand over mine and guide the quill as it made the unfamiliar lines. He—

I don't want to think of the parlor. Something unforgivable happened in that room. All I see when I think of the parlor is what I saw the night I left. It stains all the other memories. Even the happy ones—the learning, the fire that crackled in the fireplace, the meals my father and I shared.

Best to leave the past where it belongs and stay where you belong— the present. Isabelle hands me the lamp when I walk over to free up her hands.

"Thanks," she says.

I hold the lamp carefully, like a volatile dragon that I'm afraid will squirm out of my grasp and light all this gunpowder.

When Isabelle reaches back up to fool with the pulley, I see her full figure. Her long but strong body, her black hair hanging over her shoulders. The confidence in which she holds herself; a total lack of insecurity or self-doubt. You can tell a lot about a person by how they stand. She is full of fire and iron and ocean wind.

I remember when she put the captain's hat on my head and smiled. The thought makes me smile, maybe she meant something more by the gesture.

The three of us will set up our own little kingdom and live by the sea. When we've had our fill of it, we can move inland, where the natives will mistake oars for shovels. We'll buy anything we want, do anything we want, and be free. Guilt stings when I remember that Isabelle won't be coming.

Don't go getting attached, James. No place for it. You're going to ransom her over first chance you get. It's just you and Charlie. There'll be plenty of other girls; you'll have the whole African continent.

I shake my head and get back to the matter at hand.

"There," she says, "I've got it."

She ties the rope to the hatch she was working on. "You're going to love this."

She takes my arm and walks me to the bow end of the deck. Two ropes hang by the door. She pulls the starboard rope. All the cannon doors on that side open. The breeze chases the mustiness from the hull. I welcome the sound of the sea.

"I have the same system of ropes and pulleys rigged for the portside. If need be, I can open the hatches, tie off the rope, and run down the row, lighting off all the cannons. This is only good for one volley though. I could never reload the cannons by myself, but it might offer a quick strike if we need it. You and Charlie can help me load all the cannons in the morning."

She drops the rope. The doors slam shut.

"Brilliant," I say.

She smiles and brushes a strand of hair behind her ear. It reveals the angular features of her smooth face.

"I hope we don't have to use them though," I say.

"I hope the same, but just being able to open the doors might be enough to intimidate Admiral Higgins. It'll make him believe the ship is fully manned, if it appears he's having doubts. It's an intimidating thing to watch a row of doors open and loaded cannons pop out. It's not something even Admirals take lightly."

I cringe at my father's name. Should I tell her and my friends? Would it make a difference either way? I don't believe that it would. We could've ended up facing any of the brilliant admirals in the British navy.

My father is exceptionally clever, and especially cunning. I had to get it from somewhere. I consider how the plan could be soured by my father realizing I'm aboard. Last I heard, he was still looking for me. If he notices me, he may be more likely to take the *San Paulo*. But if all goes well, I won't even have to look at my father. Problems will only arise if he sees me. I'll keep my head low and the plan will play out fine.

It almost always does.

At any rate, Isabelle was right about the cannon doors. This contraption will be a huge tactical asset. It gives us something to work with in a sea battle. If need be, we could put up a fight.

We've effectively rigged this ship to sail with only three sets of hands, and enter battle if forced. Is she beautiful? No. Will the *San Paulo* glide into battle like a swan? No, she'll stagger in like a fighting rooster with iron talons. But have you ever seen a rooster in a cock-fight? I wouldn't want to fight one of those birds.

Isabelle puts her hand on my shoulder. "I know I was skeptical at first, but I'm starting to think we may have a chance at this."

"More than a chance." I smile. "We're stacking the deck in our favor."

That's the best anyone can do. Play by your own rules, with your special deck of cards. That's how you win the game. It's how Caesar became emperor and how Alexander conquered the world. They bent the rules of the established order so that they could bring their own. That gave them the advantage. It upset the status quo.

"Where do you plan for us all to go in Africa? There's an obscure French colony that I think would be perfect. It's the sort of place where, if you have enough money, they don't ask your name. They simply write Monsieur Dubois on your bill of sale. The settlement is called—"

A gunshot fires off from above deck.

"What was that?" she says.

Could a ship have found us? No, Charlie would be keeping an eye out for any unwanted company. He's high in the mast and it's a full moon tonight. He would see white sails before they came near us. Were there other pirate stowaways? No, we searched every nook and cranny of this ship after we found Gunther.

Gunther! He must have fired the shot. "Gunther must be trying to take back control of the ship."

Isabelle quickly extinguishes the lamps, straps on her sword belt, and checks the powder trap of her pistol. "James, we can't hurt him too badly. We'll still need him to be our Captain Rodriguez."

"Agreed," I say as I draw my sword.

No killing blows, but I'm going to hurt the old mutineer.

Charlie is already above deck. I hope he wasn't hurt, but even more than that, I hope Charlie doesn't do anything foolish. Or make Gunther walk the plank before I can get up there. Charlie has become overeager about these sorts of things.

Isabelle follows me up the ladder to the main deck to quell our little mutiny.

8

FIRE IN A WOOD CAGE

ON THE DECK OF THE *SAN PAULO*, CHARLIE HOLDS A LOADED pistol over a horrified Gunther. Gunther, looking equal parts terrified and confused, grovels. Charlie's hand shakes and his thumb cocks the pistol. It turns out that Charlie fired the shot, but he missed, thankfully. The bullet wedged in the center mast. That could've been Gunther's head.

"It's okay, Charlie. Just put the gun down," I say with my hand outstretched to take the gun.

"But James, he killed Mehmeh!"

"Who's Mehmeh?" Isabelle whispers to me.

"No idea."

"No, James, this villain has to die. You don't understand. He killed her, cut her up, and put her in the stew. Mehmeh never hurt anyone. She was a nice goat!" He presses the barrel of the pistol against Gunther's head. "But you wouldn't know that because you killed her!"

Gunther stutters, "The captain told me to fix dinner. With this being the eve of the day we stole the *San Paulo*, I thought stew would would be a good treat. I didn't know you had affections for the poor animal."

"An animal? Is that what you think she was? I raised her! It was my job to feed and water her. Ever since she was a little baby. She was like a friend to me before I met all of you. And some friend you turned out to be, goat killer!"

"It's okay, Charlie." *Think fast, don't let Charlie kill Gunther.* I imagine propping up a dead Gunther dressed as Rodriguez. No way—we need Gunther alive. "Charlie, when this is all over, I'll get you another goat. A whole herd of goats. Just don't kill our Captain Rodriguez surrogate."

He slowly lowers the pistol and looks toward me. "A whole herd of goats?"

"Aye, a whole herd."

"I want a black one like Mehmeh."

"Okay."

"And one of those funny ones that faint when you yell."

"I'm sure we can find one of those." I've never heard of a goat that does that, but with enough gold you can find almost anything, so sure.

Charlie uncocks the pistol, stuffs it in his belt, and huffs off. Gunther lays his head back. His whole body goes limp in relief. "Thank you, Captain. You lot are gonna be the death of me."

Isabelle laughs. "Diplomatic as King Solomon."

And treacherous as his two sons.

Gunther looks over his shoulder to make sure Charlie is out of earshot. "Might not be the best time to mention this, but dinner is ready."

Isabelle and I follow Gunther to the galley where a fire smolders in the clay oven. Knives, spoons, and pots lay scattered about in no real order. Open crates of potatoes, carrots, and other hardy vegetables suitable for sea travel line the wall.

I take a quick inventory. We'll need a lot of supplies to get us across the Atlantic when this is all over. We won't have time to make port. After stealing a massive British treasure, it's best to run away full sail.

Thankfully, Rodriguez—as in all other things—was absurdly prepared. He must have imagined the ship a fortress that might one day come under siege. Three months' worth of rations are stuffed into the galley. It's a wonder the ship still floats with all the ordinance Rodriguez crammed aboard. At any rate, we'll have plenty to get us across the Atlantic.

Isabelle sits down next to me at the wooden table. The tables are suspended from ropes attached to the ceiling. They rock with the waves. You have to hold your bowl between your elbows to keep it from getting away—an old sailor's trick.

Gunther brings the iron cauldron. He ladles the thick stew of carrots, potatoes, onion, and goat into wooden bowls.

Gunther may be many things, but he isn't a bad cook. This stew is a testament to his skill in the kitchen. I shouldn't have doubted the cook of the great Captain Rodriguez. I hadn't realized how hungry I was. We've all been up most of the night. In a few hours the sun will rise.

Isabelle guzzles her stew, ready to move onto something else. Perhaps her next project aboard the ship.

We've made all our alterations. Everything is set for our intercept tomorrow with the *Endurance*. We've rigged the sails to be manned by one person, made the gun deck operable from one rope, and we've found our Captain Rodriguez. We still have to load the cannons and dress up Gunther, but that can wait till morning.

Charlie steps through the door of the galley. Hunger drives him to reluctantly join us. Gunther timidly hands him a bowl of stew. Charlie jerks it from his hands, spilling some on the floor.

He sits down and eats. However, he picks out all the meat.

Isabelle scoops the last bit of stew from her bowl and says, "We need to go over the plan for tomorrow again."

"We've gone over it a million times," Charlie grunts.

"Yes, but there's still holes. We haven't decided who will take out their lookout. Their deck will be lower than ours, yes, so they won't be able to see that our ship is unmanned. But their lookout will. One of us will have to sneak aboard their ship on our approach, quietly remove their lookout in their crow's nest, and then sneak off when they deliver the treasure."

She looks at me. "Since Gunther will be playing Captain Rodriguez, Charlie will be manning the sails, and you're a poor swordsman, I think I should be the one to sneak aboard and take out their lookout. I'm a fast swimmer. As we get close, I'll jump into the water and sneak aboard their ship. I'll climb their rigging and silence their lookout."

I'm not sure if I'm offended, impressed, or both.

But my mind quickly turns. This could work out perfectly. While she is aboard my father's ship, we could simply tell him where she is. They can capture her, and then he can deliver the extra ransom gold with the treasure. It's flawless.

"I think that's a good plan," I say.

Gunther and Charlie nod approvingly, both happy to not be in the direct line of fire. Isabelle is best able to complete this part of the plan. She is keen with a sword and knife. She must have had a good teacher when she lived with her father. How she convinced him to allow a girl to learn swordplay is a mystery, but Isabelle is quick to get what she wants. Then again, the Governor is a forward-thinking man. He may have wanted his daughter to pursue such interests.

"So we never discussed exactly how big my share will be?" Gunther says. "And don't forget, my services as cook have been added to the bill."

"We'll make sure you get a little before we drop you off some place civilized." Charlie is still angry about the goat. "And don't get me started about your *services as our cook*."

"No, we split the treasure four ways," I say, "we're in this together." I feel a pang of guilt when I see Isabelle smiling, overjoyed to be a part of this. A secret part of her must have always romanticized being a pirate. She is reveling in the freedom. But she's about to see the gritty reality of the pirate's life when we betray her.

I continue with my speech. "Four quarters, for four pirates!"

Gunther nods approvingly and raises his tankard.

Charlie sulks before giving in. "All right. All right."

"What else needs to be done tonight, Captain?" Gunther asks.

"Nothing else tonight. Charlie, make sure we're on course and then we'll need to get some rest. When we wake up tomorrow, we'll load the cannons and dress up Gunther. We've done all we can do. We'll intercept the *Endurance* and either we'll take her, or we won't."

"Real inspirational, James," Charlie says.

Isabelle stands up. "No, after tomorrow, after we rob the *Endurance* of her British treasure, we'll be shareholders of this world. With that money we'll be free. We'll run off to some savage place to spend our fortune. We'll live in all the comforts of money. In that place, we'll be kings and I'll be a queen." She picks up her tankard. "To treasure!"

"Aye!" Gunther and Charlie raise their tankards.

Isabelle sits back down. She would've made a good pirate captain. A better one than me.

It wouldn't surprise me if she becomes a captain. She won't be in her father's care for long after we ransom her. She'll escape. That makes me feel a little better. They'll lock the doors tighter this time, but she's clever. It does no good to lock a fire in a wooden cage.

She drains her tankard, stands up, and walks out, presumably to check the rigging on her cannon doors before bed.

Gunther picks up the bowls but doesn't bother washing them. No need for such trivialities on a night of celebration. He pats me on the shoulder. "You're a good lad, James. You have the devil in you, that's for sure, but you're still a good lad."

For a moment, I wonder if he's reconsidered not liking me. It's odd the people you get dragged into caring about. Gunther nods and leaves the galley.

I'll be honest; I didn't like Charlie when I first met him—back when he spent his free hours sitting outside the brig. It felt condescending. I was angry that he was free, and I was caged. But the more he visited, the more I learned he wasn't there flaunting his freedom or giving me charity. Charlie needed a friend and no one else aboard the ship would have him. A captive audience as I may have been, I didn't try to run him off. I guess he took that as a sign of friendship.

Now that we've survived this together, I think of him as a brother. And Gunther—he's becoming that strange uncle who sputters out the occasional gem of wisdom between swigs of brandy. Your family becomes the people you live life with—those who fate conscripts to share your dream of stealing a ship or making a fortune.

Hardship creates a bond between those who endure it. Like when you're in battle and you're about to be cut to bits, but your friend saves you. That creates something deeper than friendship. Even with Isabelle— I've only known her a few days, but because of this crazy plan we've somehow survived, I look at her and—

No. No. No.

I've got to leave those thoughts. Walk away. I can't let my mind wander there. If I do, I'll reconsider. Yes, she's wonderful. Yes, she's free and beautiful. Does she deserve to be ransomed? No, but that's just the way of the world. I've made my choice when it comes to Isabelle. No going back now.

Soon, Charlie and I hear Gunther snoring from the other room.

I lean in close to Charlie and whisper, "I've got good news. The captain of the *Endurance* is friends with the Governor of Havana. After they deliver the treasure, while Isabelle is still aboard their ship, we can ransom her. Admiral Higgins will pay the ransom with the rest of the treasure."

"James, that's brilliant." Charlie leans back in his chair and touches his chin. "That'll make this simple. We'll be able to do it all at once." He taps his tankard to mine.

The plan is set, but I still feel guilty whenever I think of how happy Isabelle is aboard this ship, living this adventure, hunting this treasure, and being a pirate.

9

SOPHOCLES

I can't sleep. Too much on my mind. I'm tossing and turning as the dark ship creaks. Waves sway my hammock, churning the thoughts in my mind—the gun deck doors, the mast, loading the cannons tomorrow, making sure Gunther plays his part well, Isabelle.

Charlie and Gunther are snoring loud enough to wake the dead. I flip out of my hammock, rub my eyes, splash some water in my face, and then go above deck.

It's still a few hours to sunrise. The stars are clear, except for a few clouds. They reflect in the water like lamps floating on the sea. I walk the deck of my ship, inspecting the new rigging, making sure the hatches are stowed. But I'm not alone. Standing at the bow of the ship, feeling the wind, and watching the waves is Isabelle.

Strands of long black hair slip from her braid. Moonlight reflects in her eyes as they explore the expanse of the world.

I lean against the railing, trying to startle her. "Can't sleep either?" I say a little louder than I need to.

But the woman has nerves of steel. "No, just too excited. The more I think about it, the more I believe we can do this. I keep thinking about what it'll be like after we steal that treasure. You, me, Charlie, and I think we should consider bringing Gunther along. I didn't like him at first, but he's growing on me. Has little bits of wisdom tucked away in his mind where you wouldn't expect to find them. And he makes a good stew."

"Aye, maybe we should bring him along."

He's a bit shady, old, and greedy, but Gunther has done right by us so far.

"And I've been thinking about where we should go. There's a remote French colony on the ivory coast of Africa. My father spent time there as a child. It's called La Côte du Ciel. It's a mining town plenty large enough for us to blend into. It was supposed to house several Counts, so they built mansions there. But no one ever moved into them. The weather was too hot, the Counts said. We could buy one. The French have no interest in Spanish-British squabbles, so they'll never hear about the robbing of the *Endurance*. The best part is, the town is just seedy enough not to question how or why three adolescents are richer than the king."

"That sounds nice."

It really does. A little French town, somewhere in the wilds of Africa. I'm sure Charlie could navigate us there.

"And the best part, from what my father told me, is that the beach is white, and the ocean isn't just clear like it is here in the Caribbean, it's a perfect blue, like sapphire. That's why the French named it the coast of heaven. Do you speak any French, James?"

"I know all the swear words."

"That'll get you real far in La Côte du Ciel. Say 'bonjour.'"

"Bonjour. If you're making me say something funny, you can just stop now..."

"It means 'hello.' And your accent is terrible. Remember, the French speak through their nose. When you speak, let the sound come out of your nose by opening the back of your throat. Try this 'Mon nom est Jamie.'"

"Moan nome is Jame."

"We'll have to work on that."

"So you speak French?"

"*Oui.* And Spanish and English, and a fair bit of Latin and Greek. My father insisted." Her sentence trails off. She looks out across the sea that stretches forever in every direction, no land in sight, and then says, "Thank you, James."

I furrow my brow. "For what?"

"Helping me get out of the brig, stealing this ship, taking me on an adventure to steal treasure. With that treasure, we can run off to La Côte du Ciel and I'll never have to go back home. I think we'll all live happily there."

"Why don't you want to go back? I would give anything to be the child of Governor Cardoso."

"The life is rigid and the ceremony of everything is exhausting."

"I don't see how the life of a rich governor could be exhausting."

"And," she continues, "I had to do everything my father and mother said. I wanted to swim and walk the streets, and drink ale, but they said those things were unbecoming for a lady. I like the feel of water and the caress of wind. I could have neither of them in my father's mansion."

"That doesn't sound like the Governor Cardoso I know."

Meeting the Governor when he came to see my father changed me. Governor Cardoso was almost a divine experience. Only my father had ever looked at me like I had a soul. To the rest of the world, because of my skin, I was an object. But not to the Governor. He stood tall, his grey beard came to a sharp point at his chin. He may never have said anything to me, but he didn't look down on me, he looked straight, as though I was his equal. His glances rattled forgotten wings in my soul.

"How did you know him? Well, never mind. He kept a lot of odd friends. Did you ever come to Havana? You and I might have met as children and just don't remember. As for who my father was, you're right. He was an idealist, but even idealists can only do so much with the world they're given. He couldn't control the fact that I was a girl and that the world has certain expectations of women."

As the daughter of the governor of Havana, she could've had anything she wanted. But not even all the money in the world could buy the freedom of the sea.

"How were you captured by Captain Rodriguez?" I ask.

"He caught me when I was running away from home. I stole a small sloop from the harbor and was headed north to the British colonies. He came across me by chance and quickly realized who I was."

"So, you were a pirate even before you met me!"

Even though she didn't like the life of governor's daughter, it sounds as though she was loved. But my father, he never had time for me. He was always working on some project or some assignment. I was left alone for weeks with our nanny.

I too was cooped up in a house I didn't want to be in, longing for freedom, to make my own way in the world. I can understand why she ran away. I also know how she's feeling now. I had never felt truly free before taking this ship. With the taking of the *San Paulo*, I took hold of my own destiny.

Isabelle was experiencing something similar, a euphoria of freedom. I look over at her and she's smiling, tasting the free wind. I smile too, seeing how happy she is.

Isabelle looks up toward the sky. *"Dwell on the beauty of life. Watch the stars and see yourself running with them."*

"Marcus Aurelius," I say. She's quoting Marcus Aurelius, the Stoic Roman Emperor known for his wisdom. Marcus Aurelius never conquered kingdoms, he never led Rome to war, but he was great in his own manner.

Her head snaps toward me. "How did you know that?"

"I know how to read. My father insisted," I gently mock. "I never read Marcus Aurelius in the original Latin like you probably did, but I read the English translation."

She throws her head back and laughs. "A scoundrel who knows his ancient writings. And Suetonius? You must know of him."

"The *Twelve Caesars* is one of my favorite books."

"Plutarch? Homer? Thomas Aquinas?"

"Yes, all of them."

"You're well read. I'll admit I have another reason for running away from home. I was supposed to get married to an absolute dunce. My father wanted me to meet the man he had matched me with. I'm not sure what my father was thinking. He knows who I am and that I have no patience with fools. I tried to get to know this young man anyway. So, I quoted *Antigone* by Sophocles." She looks toward me. "Have you read *Antigone?*"

Was I receiving the same test as the young man from her story?

"I never read *Antigone*, but I did read *Oedipus Rex*."

She nods. That must've been a passing answer.

"So, I quote to him, '*Go then, if you must, but remember, no matter how foolish your deeds, those who love you will still love you.*' Then I asked him what he thought it meant. Do you know what that loggerhead said? He said, 'Why are you talking so fancy?'" She looks at me. "What do you think it means, James?"

I turn the quote in my mind. I only have a few seconds to answer before the moment is over, before she writes me off as a loggerhead like her failed suitor. "I think it means that people who really love you will love you even when you make a mistake."

"That's what I take it to mean too. Admiral Higgins told me that quote. He gave me my copy of *Antigone*. He would look me in the eye and say, '*Those who love you will still love you.*' Then he would nod toward my father and say, 'Remember that, Isabelle.'"

A tear wants to escape my eye, but I block it. My father often said the same to me. *Those who love you will still love you.*

"I think it's important to forgive. My father loved me deeply. He couldn't help it that I was a girl and that this world has a certain mold girls must be squashed into. If the world had been different, he wouldn't have had to force me into a corset. All he did, he did because he loved me. So, I'm going to forgive him. One day, I'll write him a letter telling him such, but for now, I've forgiven him. I'm no longer angry because I love him. And despite his shortcomings I will still love him."

Flawed as he might have been, Governor Cardoso was a good man. I've never questioned the relationship he and my father had. There's plenty about the governor for my father to have been drawn to. But what drew the Governor to my father? What shared secrets or plans had sealed their friendship?

All the governor did, he did for Isabelle. All my father did, he did for himself. He was away from home for his own gains, for his own promotions and glory. No doubt the plans he and the Governor made benefited him.

One day I might forgive him. I'd like to, because after forgiving her father, Isabelle has a lightness about her, like all the pieces of her world have come together. Like she lacks nothing. I'd like to feel like that too.

Anything else she wins in this life—treasure, love, power—will just be extra in addition to the peace she already owns.

Isabelle gives me the look that means she's sizing me up. Like when she was trying to decide if I could deliver the treasure or not. This time, it's a different test. She's looking for something else in the contents of my soul.

My mind had passed her tests, but would my heart?

It seems she can't decide. She turns from me, back to the ocean, and says, "I've always wanted this freedom. I'm very happy with this, James."

Then I remember what Charlie and I have planned for her.

If we hand her over, she'll die in that cage she fears so much.

No, we can't do it. The little bit of extra treasure isn't worth it. This is the sort of thing Gunther was talking about when he talked to me about overreaching. Know where to stop and know what's important. The friends we share the treasure with are more important than gaining more treasure.

We can't ransom her. I'll tell Charlie later, but Isabelle is with us for good. The four of us—Charlie, me, Isabelle, and Gunther. We'll be like a dysfunctional family, living together on the Coast of Heaven. A family brought together by a common fate and sealed by a daring crime. We'll be the sort of family each of us were looking for all our lives. Isabelle will have freedom, Gunther will have peace, Charlie will have friends. It'll be perfect.

The four of us will sing by the ocean to the tune of Charlie's violin. We'll catch fish from the water and cook them over a fire on the beach. We'll live out our days in the obscure French colony on the coast of heaven and if we get tired of there, we'll have money to visit other places.

In twenty years, we'll all have changed so much that we'll be unrecognizable. The world will have forgotten how someone stole the *San Paulo* in an audacious robbery to take the *Endurance's* treasure. If they remember, they'll remember it as a legend they tell children, not as a fact that could be brought to court.

"James? You listening to me, James?" Isabelle says. She had been talking while I was lost in my thoughts. She was saying something about the sand of Le Côte du Ciel. But I was too busy trying to figure out how to quietly undo the coup I had planned against her.

She can never know. Charlie and I will have to take this secret to our graves.

"Huh? Yeah, sorry. I was just thinking about what you were telling me about La Côte du Ciel."

She smiles. "Those will be good days for us."

"Aye, they will be."

10

SCORNED

THE SKY PAINTS ITSELF HUES OF BLUE AND ORANGE, MIXING together with the ocean. Isabelle is leaning against the railing next to me, watching a lone whale swim alongside the ship. After staring at the horizon in silence, Isabelle rolls her shoulders and tells me she's going to sleep. "Goodnight, James."

"Goodnight."

She walks off, stretching her arms to the sky. Her loose pants and shirt reveal her strong figure in the tug of the wind. When she sees me watching her climb down the hatch, she winks.

I can't believe Charlie and I even considered ransoming her. What stupidity drove us to think that was a good idea? My stomach fills with guilty wolves rumbling around. Time to fix this, quickly.

A line of sun crest appears on the horizon. I climb below deck to wake Charlie.

He and Gunther are still in their hammocks, wrapped in scratchy blankets, and snoring like dying men. Glad to see they slept well. I poke Charlie. He thrashes about, tumbles out of his hammock, and wildly swings the candle stick he had been sleeping with.

"Don't go waking a man like that, James. We're pirates now, alert at all times." He looks at the candle stick in his hand. "I could've accidentally killed you."

"Yeah. Come on, we need to talk. I've been thinking about something."

"Really? Me too."

Gunther stutters, sits up, and mumbles, "Captain, I'm sorry about the goat." He lays back down and continues muttering. "Rodriguez, I won't be doing it again. No, Captain, don't maroon me. I'll make a better stew next time." He snores.

"He does that sometimes," Charlie says. "A sleep talker, he is."

I grab Charlie's arm and pull him into the hall to avoid waking Gunther.

"I bet we've had the same thought," Charlie says. "I've been thinking it too."

"You mean it?"

"Oh yes, I don't know what we were thinking."

"Good, I'm glad you—"

"We shouldn't have eaten that stew!" Charlie jerks his thumb toward Gunther. "We should've keelhauled him for what he did to Mehmeh."

I slap my forehead. "Charlie, it was just a goat."

"Just a goat?" He looks like I've insulted his mother. "And I've been thinking about something else. We should re-name the ship. I know, I know, we're going to scuttle her when this is all done and that I shouldn't get attached. Mom never let me name the chickens because once you name something, you can't help but get attached, but hear me out. I've come up with the best name ever." He waves his hand through the air. "The *Charlie's Revenge*. Get it? Because this is how I get my revenge on Captain Rodriguez." Charlie smiles, looking hopeful.

"We've got more important things right now."

"What?"

"We can't ransom Isabelle back to her father."

"Why not? You came up with a perfect plan. It's flawless, smooth as milk. We won't have a better opportunity come along. We'll just hand her over to Admiral Higgins during the *Endurance* interception."

"No, it's not a problem with the plan…it's something else—" I lower my head.

Charlie gives me a condemning smile and elbows me. "You like her, don't you? Don't worry. I like her too. She's a delightful girl."

"And you were going to ransom her anyway?"

"I like her, but I love money." Charlie smiles a greedy grin.

I shake my head. "Anyway. We're not going to ransom her. She's going to come with us and we're going to a place called *La Côte du Ciel*. All four of us. We're going to be a strange, dysfunctional family, cook dinners together, and be free men and woman. It's going to be great, trust me on this, Charlie. I know you don't like Gunther yet, but he's growing on me and he'll grow on you too. Okay?"

"La what?"

"It's French—a mining colony on the ivory coast. We're all going there after we steal the *Endurance*'s treasure."

"Ah. Whatever you say, Captain. I've liked all the French people I've met. Well, they didn't speak English and I don't speak French, so I guess there was no way to really tell if they liked me or not, but I liked them. Will not speaking French be a problem?"

"No, Isabelle can teach you. Now listen closely." I snap my fingers in Charlie's face. "This is really important. Charlie, we can never speak of this again. Isabelle can never know. Swear to me, we'll never speak of this again."

"That goes without saying, Captain. I'll take your secrets into my grave. She won't hear this from ol' Charlie." Charlie nonchalantly leans against the wall. "I can't imagine how peeved she'd be if she ever found out we had planned to ransom her to her father."

"You're going to do what?!" A female voice from behind me shouts. She walks over and slams the open palm of her hand against Charlie's shoulder, knocking him back.

I start to shake and I my stomach drops. My throat swells. I turn around to see Isabelle with one hand on her pistol and the other balled into a fist.

"We're not going to do anything," I say.

"I heard what Charlie said. The two of you are going to ransom me back to my father!" She draws the pistol and then her sword.

"No, we're not!"

"That's not what Charlie just said." She points the gun at Charlie.

Charlie holds his hands up. "No, you misheard me. We *were* going to ransom you back to your father, now we've decided not to! Isn't that great? James likes you too much to do that. And we're all going to go to that La Cot place!"

He smiles like he believes the whole situation will resolve all because we considered treason, planned treason, but stopped right before we stabbed her in the back because we like her.

"You swine." Isabelle spits and turns to leave.

I run after her and touch her arm. "We just thought—"

She turns back and lays her cutlass across my neck. "Thought what? Thought I was some stupid girl to be used as a pawn in your game of treasure? That I was an item to be sold? That I didn't have a soul and a love of the wind like you do?" Her face is twisted in lines of anger, hurt, and broken trust.

Her blade nips my neck, like a scratch. Her eyes are narrowed—you can see the anger there. But her lower lip trembles slightly—there you can see the hurt.

"You two really are pirates," she says.

She lifts her cutlass and sheaths it but doesn't stow the pistol.

I feel my neck. A drop of blood drips from where the cutlass touched me. The blood smears my fingers, making them sticky, incriminating them.

She stomps through the hull of the ship to the main deck. Charlie and I follow her, both of us making frantic apologies.

"I don't know why you're so mad, Isabelle," Charlie says. "It's not like we actually went through with our plan. We only considered it!"

The horizon is a flaming hearth. The clouds are smoke. The sun is rising out of the ocean. Not all the water in the sea could put out those flames. The deck is painted orange like the fires of Isabelle's anger.

We follow her to the captain's cabin. It only has one door. One way in or out. She stomps across the deck, her head held high in angry dignity.

"I'm sorry, Isabelle," I say.

"Don't speak to me again. You're not sorry for what you've done. You're sorry because I caught the two of you in the middle of your stupid plans. You're the ones who are lucky. Think about it: what do you think would've happened if you told Admiral Higgins I was aboard his ship? I would have yelled out that there's only three of you aboard the *San Paulo*. I would have told the Admiral to open fire—that we'd dressed a cook up as the old captain, and that he should sink the *San Paulo*. That the whole thing was a farce! I would have been captured, but I would have at least had the pleasure of watching you be blown to smithereens and go down in flames!"

Isabelle is still patching the holes in our broken plans. I hadn't considered all that when I told Charlie of the original plan to ransom Isabelle. She's right, once we announced that she was on board the *Endurance*, she would have known we had betrayed her. They would've captured her, that is certain, but she would have had her revenge.

"Isabelle, wait," Charlie says.

She stops in the wooden doorway and looks back over her shoulder. "What?"

"Are you still going to help us tomorrow? You know, steal the treasure from the *Endurance*?"

Her eyes widen in shocked anger at Charlie's pigheadedness. She slams the heavy wooden door in his face. The latch thunks behind it and we're left standing on the deck like fools.

Charlie shakes his head. "Women."

"Don't you see what we've done? She's scorned! I can't believe we did that. What were we thinking?"

"Gold."

"I know what we were thinking about, Charlie, but why?" I lay my head against the door. "I'm sorry, Isabelle."

No answer.

A distant thought wanders into my mind. One that doesn't belong there in a moment like this. I think of Marcus Arulieus, about his writings on wisdom and honor. I had read his writing but missed the point. He warned against greed, as had Gunther, but did Charlie or I listen? No, we just went on chasing an extra bit of gold in exchange for the bondage of another.

We were no better than those who stole my mother from Africa and sold her.

"Come on, Charlie, nothing more we can do tonight."

I motion for Charlie to follow me below deck to the barracks. We can't do anything to fix this now. And I need some rest.

I locate the hammock that we had agreed was mine. Laying in it is a book bound in a hard leather cover. I open it and thumb through the pages, wafting the smell of old paper to my nose. The cover is written in Greek.

A note falls from the leafs of paper. In Isabelle's small, neat handwriting, is a short message, *"I found this among the captain's books. It's a copy of Antigone. It's in Greek, but don't worry, I'll teach you. If you want to learn. —Isabelle"*

The old book weighs more in my hand than it should, like a cannon ball or a shackle. This is why she was in the hallway when Charlie and I were talking. She had come to drop the book off in the barracks before going to bed.

"James, do you think this hurts my chances with her?"

I don't give Charlie's question the dignity of an answer. I set the book on a barrel next to my hammock. "We'll talk to her when we wake up."

Charlie covers himself in a blanket. "If she doesn't slit our throats while we're sleeping."

Knowing Isabelle, that is a real possibility.

11

FATE GOES AS IT MUST

I ROLL OUT OF MY HAMMOCK AROUND NOON. I FEEL EXHAUSTED and need another few days of sleep. But we have work to do before our intercept of the *Endurance*.

The water basin in the crew's quarters is open. Gunther must already be up, but Charlie is still contorted in his hammock, hugging his blanket. I splash water in my face and put on my loose shirt, pants, and Rodriguez's boots. The thick weapon belt feels heavier on my shoulder than yesterday. I stuff my pistols in their holsters and my sword in its sheath. The captain's hat lays on the barrel next to my bed. I pick it up and see the copy of *Antigone*.

I put the hat back down but stop. I'm captain even when I've messed up. A good captain makes up for his mistakes. I put on the hat.

"Charlie, wake up." I poke his hammock.

He swats me away and rolls over.

I stumble to the galley. Charlie tips out of his hammock and drags behind me. We walk in on Gunther cooking breakfast. Today he's got a spring to his step—the kind men get when they know they'll be rich by the end of the day. And if all goes to plan, we'll all be extraordinarily rich. So he's as merry as the day is long.

He stretches, exposing his big round belly. "What a great night last night. After dinner, I slept like a baby. I think I conked out before the rest of you. Bet the three of you were partying all night. Heh. In my younger years, I was quite the scoundrel. You boys have a good night?"

Charlie groans and lays his head on the table.

"Alright, alright. Young people never feel good when they have to wake up early. Well, not that it's early. It's near mid-afternoon. But you boys had a busy night. Anyway, here's your breakfast. You'll feel better after that."

He places two plates of cured ham and hard sea biscuits before us. Charlie tucks in and devours the meat. He's hungry after having picked out most of his stew last night. I nibble at the food, too busy thinking about how to make things right with Isabelle.

As if she sensed me thinking about her, she walks into the galley. She's wearing fresh clothes, a bandana around her forehead, and an extra pistol stuffed in her belt. Her extra armaments send a clear message. She's still mad and has no intention of trusting us.

"Good morning, m'lady," Gunther says.

"Good morning, Gunther."

She doesn't look at us.

She sits at the opposite end of the table, as far away from Charlie and I as she can get. Gunther brings her a plate. The metal plate clicks down in front of her. She cuts the ham with her knife, probably imagining it's my face.

She smiles and says, "Thank you, Gunther." Then she casts Charlie and I a daggered look.

Gunther's head is ducked. His eyes dart between Isabelle, Charlie, and I, sensing her resentment and my guilt.

"Glad to see we're one big happy family this morning." He takes a seat near the middle of the table, trying to be some sort of mediator, but it doesn't do any good. Isabelle switches between smiling when facing Gunther to scowling when she looks at Charlie and me.

Gunther fidgets awkwardly in the silence, chewing his bread a little louder than necessary. He eyes the three of us uneasily.

Finally, Isabelle speaks. "Charlie, are we still on course to intercept?"

Charlie snaps to attention. "Yes, I checked before I went back to bed last night."

"After breakfast check again. Will we still make it there by this afternoon?"

"Yes."

Charlie opens his mouth to say something more. He thinks there might be something more he was supposed to say, but the silence beats him back. He closes his mouth. Gunther looks uncomfortable. I think part of him is relieved that we're mad at each other instead of at him for killing the goat.

"We need to talk about the plan," Isabelle says.

Gunther and Charlie let out a deep, relieved breath. Gunther may not have known the problem, but he could tell our haggard alliance was strained.

I'm relieved too, but still apprehensive. She's still going to help us, but she certainly isn't happy about it.

Isabelle swallows a bite of bread then says, "I won't be the one to go aboard the *Endurance* to silence their lookout. One of you will have to do it."

Her reasoning behind this is obvious. She doesn't trust us not to abandon her while she's still onboard the ship.

"And when this is all over, I want you to drop me off at Tortuga. I'll be going my separate way with my share of the treasure after that."

"What's wrong, m'lady?"

I never knew Gunther to be the consoling sort. But his voice is warm, almost fatherly in its tone of concern.

"Nothing. I've just reconsidered my options and goals for after we complete our mission. I would simply rather go somewhere else." But she glares at me when she says it.

"Alright, alright. I won't pry no deeper, but in my years of sailing, I've see spats like this tear crews apart. You all be mindful not to let it affect your work." Gunther stands up, takes the dishes, and leaves the galley.

"Don't go far, Gunther," Isabelle yells as he leaves, "we've got to turn you into Rodriguez before long."

"Yes, ma'am."

She turns her attention to Charlie and me. "And you two, check our course then load the cannons."

"Aye, Captain," Charlie says sarcastically.

Wrong choice, mate. Charlie's about to get the verbal beating of a lifetime.

She shoots to her feet.

Even when Charlie is standing straight and tall, Isabelle holds five inches on him. She glares at him and he cowers into his seat. "You two need to decide who's going aboard the *Endurance*."

Time to try for an apology. "Isabelle, Charlie and I are sorry. We made a mistake and—"

"Let me stop you there. Are you speaking to me about the plan?"

"No."

"Are you speaking to me about an issue related to the ship or our expedition?"

"No."

"Then you have no reason to speak to me. That will be all." She walks out and slams the door behind her.

"I blame you for this, Charlie," I say.

"Me? Why me? What did I do?"

"'Let's just drop Isabelle off in Havana for ransom, James. It'll be easy, James. We'll get lots of gold, James.'"

"And what did you say when I proposed the idea? Were you morally indignant? Did you turn your nose up at me and say, *'No, Charlie, we can't just sell off the pretty lass? That would be wrong; we're good pirates.'* No, I think your exact words were *'you and me.'*"

"You need to fix this, Charlie."

"What do you want me to do? Jump in the ocean and pick some flowers for her? Or have you forgotten that Isabelle isn't the sort who likes flowers and sonnets, that she's the sort who enjoys cold, hard revenge!"

Gunther pokes his head through the door. "She gone?"

"Aye," Charlie says.

"I don't know what you boys pulled, but that's a scorned woman. You two have royally messed up. Ain't seen a woman that mad since I was last in Tortuga and I tried to leave without paying for her services— Never you mind the last time I saw a woman this angry. But it was bad. Nearly lost a piece of myself. You'll want to do something about this. Best to make right with Isabelle. For all you boys know, she'll sell you out. She strikes me as the sort of would take pleasure in that sort of thing. She might be to the point where she don't mind going down in a blaze of glory, so long as she drags you two down with her. Might want to try and make things right before we go into this whole thing with the *Endurance*. It's a boogered up plan as is. It can't handle any mavericks or scorned women."

"Gunther! Where are you?" Isabelle yells from another room.

"Welp, looks like I'm overdue for my appointment with the hairdresser. Wish me luck, boys! Remember: fix this." He leaves to follow the sound of Isabelle's voice.

Typical Gunther; offer advice, but no way to enact that advice. Just how are we going to get Isabelle to forgive us? We decided not to hand her over, that should count for something, but apparently not.

"You got any bright ideas on how to fix this?" I ask.

Charlie shrugs his shoulders. "I'm tapped out of ideas. Too tired to think now anyway and we've got a long day ahead of us."

"Alright then, well, which of us is going to go aboard the *Endurance* and remove the lookout? We can at least settle that."

Charlie crosses his arms. "Not me."

"Well, I certainly don't want to go."

"We'll flip your lucky coin for it. I call heads."

"No."

"Just flip the coin."

I pull the gold doubloon from my pocket and frown. With a flick of my thumb it's in the air. It spins like a little gold sun before I catch it in my hand.

It's heads.

Not a lucky coin today.

Charlie smiles. "I couldn't have gone anyway. I've got to be aboard the *San Paulo* to manage the sails and navigation. That leaves you, James." Charlie shrugs his shoulders. "I'm sure you'll do fine."

I'll have to sneak aboard my father's ship, climb the mast in broad daylight, and silence their watchman. Son infiltrates his father's ship. I suppose this is how it was meant to happen.

"I'm going to go check the rigging one last time." Charlie pats my shoulder then walks out of the galley, leaving me alone with Gunther's mess of a kitchen.

Of course it would be me boarding my father's ship.

Fate isn't content to keep you a stone's throw away from the people you never thought you'd see again. No, it wants you to get close enough for them to see how much facial hair you've grown since running away.

God, help me.

If my father catches me aboard the ship, or even catches sight of me, he'll give chase to the *San Paulo*—even if he believes it to be fully armed. He wants me to come home that badly. He still loves me that much, I believe.

Fathers love in odd ways—sometimes they love even more fiercely than mothers. Especially men like my father who no longer have the mother of their sons. Fathers are just broken men trying to do right by their children. They get lost easily. They get too focused on a means of income or position of power.

I'm sure he started with pure intentions before he disappeared. I'm sure all he wanted was to make enough money and have enough position to give me a good life. But that isn't what it turned into. All the time he spent with the Governor of Havana, that wasn't related to work. That was purely for pleasure or some other personal gain. Time he could have spent at home.

Even without worrying about being caught by my father, I'm still left with the lookout. If I learned anything from when we stole the *San Paulo* last night, it's that I am not a master swordsman.

I've never killed anyone or thrown them from a ship's rigging. The thought turns my stomach. For all my thoughts of treasure and wanting to take it regardless of the cost, I worry about what I'll do when I climb into that crow's nest.

I can't kill him, and I have no idea how I'll go about subduing him.

You're forced to learn some things as you go.

Time to help Charlie adjust our course then load the cannons.

12

THE ENDURANCE

From the bridge of the *San Paulo*—where Charlie is plotting our course—the sky is as blue as the sea is clear. The sun glimmers in the water. It forces me to adjust my captain's hat to shield my eyes. The wind blows at a steady pace, keeping our open sail stretched smooth.

The calm day is a liar. It's deceiving itself about what's to come. A storm brews, not in the sky, but on the deck of a ship. A hurricane, silently turning, ready to take the *Endurance*.

The *San Paulo* is the storm and the *Endurance* is the unsuspecting village, enjoying the fleeting sun of a day soon to end.

Or so I hope.

Charlie crouches beside me, bent over a compass and map, making his calculations.

"How much longer?" I ask.

"Just you wait. This is delicate business." He points a compass accusingly at me.

"Alright, alright." I prop myself up on the ornate railing overlooking the deck.

The carvings along the wood are cracked and pocketed with bullet holes. You can still decipher the leafy swirls cut into the wood by a master carpenter. Wouldn't surprise me if Rodriguez stole this ship from royalty. It sets a perfect scene for the Devil King, Queen, and two Knights. The Queen leans over the bow of the ship, one hand holding a rope; the other holding a spyglass over the *San Paulo*'s figurehead.

For most ships, the figure head is a mermaid, a dragon, or some other beast from mythology. The *San Paulo* is not your typical ship. At the bow is a carving of Captain Rodriguez, parting the waves before the ship with his hands. No one ever accused Rodriguez of modesty or moderation.

Isabelle stands with her back to us, watching the horizon line, partly because she's still angry and partly because she's scouring for any sign of the *Endurance*. We're not due to intercept for several hours. But we have much left to do before our grand bluff.

Gunther also moves about the deck—half dressed in his Rodriguez costume. He's gotten his hair combed, oiled, and wrapped into a clean ponytail. Isabelle cleverly powdered his face to make him a shade darker, and to hide his gaping pores. She's giving him a break before stuffing him into the corset.

He drags out a box of rifles and sets them along the railing. Our plan is to make it look as though men are holding them behind cover. It's not the most convincing deception, but the sight of thirty rifles is intimidating—so long as Admiral Higgins doesn't realize there's no one holding the rifles. That won't happen if I can silence his lookout.

On to more pressing matters. I've yet to take the wheel of the *San Paulo*. Tonight, she will have been in my command for an entire day. I still haven't so much as touched the wheel. Which isn't that odd really now that I think about it. Traditionally, steering the ship is the job of the helmsman, but my ascent to Captain has been anything but traditional. I wrap my fingers around the worn pegs, and run my hand over the spokes inside, feeling them before gently turning.

"Hold up, James." Charlie writes some calculations on the paper he's pressed to the deck. "Alright, now, turn three points starboard and then tie the wheel. We'll reach the island within the hour."

"Aye."

It's hard to let go of the wheel. I like steering my ship, but there'll be plenty of time for leisurely sailing while crossing the Atlantic after this is all over. As soon as we loot the gold, we'll be eastward bound.

I tie off the wheel. If Charlie is right, our rendezvous with the *Endurance* is approaching. Once we're near the islands, we'll circle about the area and wait. The *San Paulo* will be positioned right in the middle of the *Endurance*'s course. They'll come right to us.

At the bow of the ship, Isabelle stows the spyglass in her belt, satisfied that the *Endurance* won't appear on the horizon for a little while longer. She's walking across the deck, her boots clicking as she moves. Gunther pauses and lowers his head as she passes.

She climbs the stairs to the bridge, her eyes still as cold as ice. She addresses Charlie and me. "Have you two loaded the cannons yet? No? What have you been doing all morning? Playing cards? Have you seen how many cannons are down there? It will take the rest of the afternoon and I'm certainly not doing it. And you'll need to load both the starboard and port cannons. We don't know which side we'll intercept from." She walks off without waiting for a reply, simply expecting us to follow her orders without question.

If you walk like a king, people will believe you're destined to wear the crown. And Isabelle walks like a king.

Isabelle yells, "Gunther! Time for dress up."

"Yes, ma'am." Gunther groans, but follows Isabelle into the Captain's cabin.

Charlie lowers his eyebrows and cuts me a disapproving glance. "She the captain now?"

"Stow that talk. Let's just get those cannons loaded."

I open the deck hatch and Charlie climbs down into the labyrinth of gunpowder and cold iron. I follow him down the ladder to the stuffy deck below.

"Think it would hurt to let in some air?" Charlie asks.

I pull the rope attached the doors on the starboard side. The pulleys creak. The way Isabelle has rigged it, lifting the doors is easy. Cool air pours in as I tie off the rope.

I lift the doors on the port side and Charlie says, "That's nearly as brilliant as what I managed with the sails."

"She's a clever one."

As was fore-mentioned, the old captain was paranoid. Charlie and I move along footpaths that curve through canyons of gunpowder and pyramids of cannonballs. If it weren't for these pathways left by the previous crew, Charlie and I could never have even gotten near the cannons.

My shoulders droop when I see the rows of cannons. They've multiplied since last night. Now I can see them in the daylight pouring through the hatches in dusty beams. Forty cannons point to sea and Isabelle was right—it'll take all afternoon.

Loading cannons is dirty business.

Charlie throws his head back and groans as he counts the cannons. "You know, it's still not too late to ransom her over, or at the very least throw her overboard."

I want to laugh, but I say, "Don't talk like that. She'll hear you."

"You're right. Best hold off on to that sort of talk. The woman has voodoo powers. Can hear through walls and see into your soul."

"And bewitch men with her charms," I say.

"She's a down right gypsy. Bet she's got voodoo dolls of each of us, ready to prick our backs and make us writhe."

Stomping thuds from the ceiling, loosing dust from its resting place to fall like snow. "I can hear you, Charlie!" Isabelle's voice is dulled by the wood slats separating the gun deck from the captain's cabin above. Her words are sharp.

Charlie eeks, then whispers, "I told you, James. Gypsy powers."

I've never loaded a cannon before. I know, it's an embarrassment—a pirate captain who has never loaded a cannon or killed a man, who can't navigate, or properly duel with swords or a pistol. We do our best with what we have. All I happen to have is my mind. But the mind isn't a muscle that can load cannons.

Loading a cannon isn't the sort of thing you want to do incorrectly. But Charlie "read a book" on firearms that included a chapter on cannons and other artillery.

"I think I know how to load these. Just drop in a sack of powder, then the ball, stuff it all in, and add a fuse. Easy. There's nothing to it really." He pauses. "Or I could be completely wrong and we're going to blow the ship to hades when and if we light these monsters. Toss of a coin really."

Isn't everything? "Comforting," I say.

"Hand me a powder packet. They're in that crate over there."

"Charlie, you need to understand that down here, 'that crate over there' could refer to twenty different crates."

"The one right next to you."

I pry open the lid. Inside are malleable cloth sacks filled with gunpowder.

It sets your heart to pumping when you're holding enough gunpowder to blow your face off. I'm careful with it, walking slowly, keeping it as far away from my body as possible, making sure that I don't drop it.

I gently place it in the palm of Charlie's waiting hand and he yells "BOOM!"

I jump back, and he laughs.

"Lighten up, Captain. This is the safe part. Firing them is where things will be…interesting."

He takes the sack of powder and slips it into the muzzle of the cannon. The inside of the barrel is too rough for it to slide all the way down. He pushes it the rest of the way with the ramrod.

"Alright, time for the cannonball."

I take one off the top of the many pyramids erected about the gun deck. I never would have guessed something so small could be so heavy. The same can be said for many things, I suppose, thinking about Isabelle and my father and the complex web of emotions people share.

I stagger over to Charlie and hand him the cannon ball. He lugs it into the muzzle and it rolls right down. It lands with a soft thud against the gunpowder at the bottom. I hand him the ramrod. He shoves it down to ensure the shot is firmly packed. A mis-packed cannon can explode.

"You can do the honor." Charlie hands me the fuse, a thick bit of twine that inserts into a small hole at the rear of the cannon.

I carefully place the fuse. One cannon loaded.

Only another thirty-nine to go.

We meticulously load each cannon in the gun deck. I lose track of the time. My arms droop a little lower with each cannon ball I carry. I should be saving my strength for when I have to climb aboard the *Endurance*. But it's essential that the cannons be loaded, even if we hope not to use them.

Several hours later, the ship is ready to blow a hole in a Spanish armada.

Or itself.

One way or another, it's going to blow up something.

Charlie and I sit down to wipe the sweat from our brows. We sip water from a barrel in the corner.

"We could blow up all of Europe with these cannons," Charlie says between slurps.

I lay back against a stack of cannon wadding and close my eyes. Not much longer. Only a few more hours until this is finished. Then I can rest properly. I'll sleep on piles of gold and go to bed wearing a crown.

I let out a deep breath to steady myself for what's coming.

As if she knew we were taking a break from work and wanted to crack the whip, Isabelle sticks her head through the hatch in the ceiling. "Get up you two!"

I'm relieved to see her smiling.

"Sails! Gunther and I have caught sight of the *Endurance*!"

13

SWIM FAST

THE *ENDURANCE* IS A MAN OF WAR SPECIALLY COMMISSIONED BY the Crown. The only one of her class. She was built to carry valuable cargo, to move fast and hit hard. She's the smallest warship the British ever constructed. But they stuffed her with as many cannons as she could carry and still float. That's why she sits so low in the water. Her two decks of guns are an intimidating feature. One row of cannons sits on the main deck, the other on the gun deck below.

The Man of War approaches from the West. We beat her to the intercept so she's coming to us. The four of us stand silently on the bridge of the *San Paulo*, all worried that a single word might spook our prey.

"Here." Isabelle hands me her telescope.

"Thank you."

With the help of the spy glass, I watch the *Endurance* cut across the ocean. I see her three masts, sails bulged with wind. The smooth curve of the ship, the planks fastened together with pitch and wood, the lattice of ropes and nets strung across the hull. Her navy blue paint is fresh and the white stripes are like bands of snow.

Unlike the *San Paulo*—which is lumbering like a lame dugong because we're only using the middle sail—the *Endurance* glides, fully manned and expertly sailed.

When you see a ship at a distance, moving into port, or barreling toward you, you suddenly realize how large they are, and, how small you and your carefully laid plans are. Ships are less like manmade vessels and more like a god or the wind. You are a mere mortal.

I give the eyeglass to Charlie. "Keep a sharp eye on her."

He nods.

"Should we raise the black, Captain?" Gunther asks. He's holding two flags. One in each hand. The British flag with its crisscrossing blue lines in one, and in the other, a black pirate flag.

"We'll fly the royal flag for now."

"Aye, Captain."

Gunther hobbles to the stern of the ship, still struggling to breathe in his costume, much less move. He hooks the flag to the mainstay and hoists.

The British flag waves like a friendly hand.

If the *Endurance* senses anything amiss, she could change her course, turn to the wind, and run. We could never give chase. Being fully crewed, the *Endurance* is far more maneuverable than us.

If she runs, we've lost her.

That's why Gunther raised the British flag. We have to pose as friends to get the *Endurance* close.

Then we raise the black.

Isabelle, true to her word—even if we weren't true to ours—did a great work on Gunther. He looks nothing like himself. He's a perfect copy of Captain Rodriguez. He would probably fool Rodriguez's own mother. If you'd never seen the captain in real life, the costume is plenty convincing. The look Isabelle gave him fits all the wanted posters.

Gunther's hair is smoothed back into a clean ponytail. A plumed hat sits on his head. She dressed him in the long, dulled maroon seaman's coat the captain was famous for wearing. The one with the gold filigree on the cuffs and trim. His boots are shined, and his shirt is clean. A bandolier of pistols is strung across his chest. Most impressive of all is the goat's hair beard plastered across his face.

"As long as he doesn't have to do too much talking, things should go smoothly," Isabelle says.

She must've seen me admiring her handiwork.

"You did good," I say.

She ignores my compliment. "I've done the best I could to help him adopt a Spanish accent like Rodriguez's, but Gunther's English is... especially thick."

I nod. At least she's talking to me again. That's an improvement from this morning.

"Charlie, what's the status on the *Endurance*?" I ask.

He keeps his eyes glued to the rapidly approaching ship. "They haven't adjusted their course. They believe we're fellow Brits."

The *Endurance* is closing in, she'll come along side us if she doesn't adjust her course. This is a tricky bit—getting her close enough so she can't run when we raise the black flag.

As the *San Paulo* approaches the intersect, I see men moving about the *Endurance*'s deck, going on with their work, unsuspecting of the approaching ship. A few pause by the railing as they walk by. They turn to us. Hopefully they won't notice that only three youngsters are looking back.

"How much longer?" Gunther stands at the ready with Rodriguez's pirate flag.

Not much longer, almost there. The timing must be perfect.

When the *Endurance* crosses the threshold of what I estimate to be close enough, I turn to Gunther. "Hoist the black."

"Aye, sir."

He lowers the British flag. In its stead, he clips Rodriguez's to the line and pulls. As it catches wind the flag reveals its full form. A solid black canvas with a white skull and catholic cross embossed above two crossed pistols.

Charlie clutches the rope he can pull to drop the sails. He's jumpy, prepared to run at the first sign of aggression by the *Endurance*.

We have the stronger wind. If he were to drop the sails, the *San Paulo* would pick up enough speed to run.

But we won't be running today.

I put my hand on his shoulder. "This is how fortunes are won, Charlie."

I fiddle with my lucky Spanish doubloon. I'm nervous too. I try not to show it. My heart would shake from my chest if it wasn't caged by flesh and bone. My hands are cold despite the Caribbean heat. I shiver.

"The *Endurance* is adjusting her course!" Gunther cries.

"Is she running?" I drop my doubloon into my pocket.

"No," Gunther pauses, and his arms drop. "God help us."

"What's happening?" Charlie asks.

"She's turning to broadside us!"

The *Endurance* slows. She's turning. Every single one of her starboard cannons are locked on us. The *San Paulo* is moving straight toward the *Endurance*. Cannon fire will rip down the length of the ship, splinter wood, light our massive stores of gunpowder, kill us, and send the *San Paulo* to the bottom of the sea.

"This is over, James. We have to run," Gunther says. "It was a clever plan, but we knew all along that we stood no chance if they made this move. We've got to get out of their line of fire, we won't survive a full volley from those guns! Drop the sails, Charlie!"

"He's right." Charlie tightens his grasp around the rope to loose the main sails. He's ready to pull.

I ignore them. Something is amiss. I feel it in my bones. I sense it in the air. The *Endurance* is stretching her Starboard to us, showing her cannons. Yet I don't believe the *Endurance* is truly prepared to engage. Something carried by the wind or read in the glittering rays of sun tells me the truth. The *Endurance* is bluffing.

After crafting our grand bluff, I recognize one when I see it.

Or I could be wrong. Perhaps Admiral Higgins is ready to kill the infamous Rodriguez de Medina.

"Captain!" Gunther says, "we need to make sail and get out of here!"

"He's right, James. We'll be killed if we don't," Charlie says. "Give the word and I'll drop the sails. We have the wind. With the extra sails we can outrun them. There's a thousand islands where we can hide."

I look to Isabelle. She focuses on my face. She senses the question I'm asking her with my eyes. *Run or bluff back?* Her face is stoic, clear, and most of all, resolved.

She nods.

Bluff back.

My eyes dart between her, Gunther, and Charlie. They want to run.

She wants to see this through. Two to one. I'll flip for it. I take my lucky doubloon. Heads we return the bluff; tails we run.

I toss the coin in the air. As it spins, Charlie yells, Gunther covers his face, and Isabelle smiles a knowing smile. I snatch the coin and flip it onto the back of my hand.

Heads.

Before Gunther can stop me, I push Charlie from behind the wheel. I grip the pegs and turn hard.

Gunther and Charlie stagger as the ship jerks onto a new trajectory. Isabelle, surefooted as ever, remains steady. She knew what was coming. I spin the wheel. The *San Paulo* swings starboard. All our broadside cannons face the *Endurance*.

"Captain, what the blazes are you doing?" Gunther yells.

We're parallel with the *Endurance*, as if we're prepared to engage in a proper sea battle. "We're not running. Isabelle, to the gun deck. Open the cannon hatches on my mark. Charlie, position yourself above the gun deck to relay my orders to Isabelle. Gunther, get ready to play Captain Rodriguez."

Isabelle doesn't question the orders. She scampers across the deck to the gun deck hatch.

"You're mad, Captain." Gunther adjusts his feathered hat and stands erect.

Charlie grabs my arm. He pulls me around to face him. "James, this is over. We can't fight them. This is insane."

"We're not going to fight. They're bluffing."

He looks across the blue sea and sees the *Endurance* opposite to us. Her gun deck doors stare at us like Methuselah eyes.

"How do you know for sure?"

"I just do." I pause. "Get ready to relay my orders to Isabelle."

Reluctance permeates Charlie's voice. "Aye, Captain." He runs to the hatch to position himself to shout my orders to Isabelle below.

"You're made of iron, James. Doubt even Rodriguez would be mad enough to try this."

"Thank you, Gunther."

"Wasn't exactly a compliment." He spits and turns toward the *Endurance*.

"Isabelle! Open the cannon hatches, now! Fire a single warning shot!"

Charlie relays my words below deck. I hear and feel the pulleys grinding beneath my feet. The gun deck doors clink open. A cannon fires beneath me. The shockwave rattles through the ship. A blur of a cannon ball splashes into the ocean past the *Endurance*'s bow.

I grasp the wheel, preparing to cling to something, in case I'm wrong and the *Endurance* opens fire. If they do, they'll blast our ship to pieces. We'll be sent to the grave in a fiery explosion engulfed by the ocean.

I close my eyes and brace for impact. All I hear is the whisper of the wind. All I felt is the sway of the sea.

They're not returning fire.

The *Endurance*'s gun deck doors chink shut. Their British flag is lowered by the steersman.

I'm anxious to see its replacement.

"They're raising the white flag, Captain." Gunther wipes the sweat from his forehead. He lets out as deep a breath as he can in his corset. "Dear Lord, I can't believe it, but you were right. They were bluffing. They had no intention of an actual fight. How did you know?"

Because I am my father's son. I thought I sensed their bluff on the wind or in my bones. I was wrong. The whispers came from the blood passed down from my father. I knew because I would have tried the same bluff before surrendering to a fight I knew I couldn't win. I knew because I am like my father. I don't tell Gunther this. I shrug my shoulders and say, "I just knew."

"Humph." Gunther shakes his head and turns away. He's getting himself into character for the big show.

The *Endurance* raises her sails. She gently moves toward us. Once she was a warship I greatly feared. Now, she's like an animal coming to slaughter.

Animals are most dangerous when cornered.

"Slow us down, Charlie," I say.

Charlie runs to the middle mast of the ship. He pulls a rope limply swinging in the wind. It's the rope he rigged to loose our one open sail. The rope falls like a cut vine. The white sail is loosed. Like a butterfly, it flutters, unsure which direction to go. It decides on the ocean. The sail floats past the ship and lands in the sea like a giant sheet in a wash bin.

The *San Paulo*'s momentum slows, but we should still reach the *Endurance*.

Isabelle rejoins us on the bridge and winks at me. She approves. Perhaps this is how I can earn her forgiveness. Charlie follows close behind her and looks a bit shaken, but he's forced himself steady.

Isabelle checks over her shoulder to judge the *Endurance*'s distance. "We've still got a few moments. Gunther, when we're within shouting distance, make our demands clear and keep negotiations short. Tell them you know how much gold is on their ship and that we want it delivered to the smallest island of that arpeggio. Then they must leave."

"I'll do my best, m'lady."

"No, '*I will do my best, señorita*' You're pretending to be a Spaniard. Keep the accent tight and your vowels short. Try not to sound like the full-blooded Englishman you are."

He shrugs. "We are what we are."

"Not today we're not. Whatever we once were, today we are pirates about to win the biggest score of their lives. I'll be below deck, ready to open the gun deck doors and fire the cannons if need be. That'll be a last resort though. Charlie, you'll need to loose the sails and get us out of here the second you hear cannon fire. It's every man for himself after that, even if they're not aboard the ship. Sorry, James."

We are pirates after all.

"I understand," I say.

"James, you'll have to get to the *Endurance* before we do and take out their lookout. Here, take this." She hands me a blue handkerchief. "If something goes wrong while you're in the crow's nest, if you think the Admiral is on to our plan, wave this so that Charlie can see it. We'll open the gun deck doors and try a bit of intimidation. But you'll have to deal with the lookout first. If you don't silence him before we reach the *Endurance*, they'll see our bluff."

"Do you have any grand advice on how I can do that? How I can reach the *Endurance* before the *San Paulo* does?" I take off my hat and hand it to Charlie.

The boats are moving faster than I expected. I remove the heavy belt from my shoulder, my shirt, and then unlatch my boots. The sun warms my skin as I prepare for the swim. I throw a coil of rope over my shoulder and strap a sheathed dagger to my leg and—

With both hands, Isabelle pushes me in the chest, over the railing. I scrape against the side of the ship as I fall. Before I crash into the water I hear her say, "My advice: swim fast, James."

14

SURRENDER

Saltwater chokes my throat and scours my nose. Beneath me is the blur of a coral reef; above me the suspended sun rays dance with the waves. As I swim up, a school of fish darts around me. Several ram into my bare chest before swaggering off. I break the surface with a cough and I gasp for air.

I turn a quick circle to gain a sense of my surroundings. The *San Paulo* lumbers past me. I swim to avoid her undertow. I wipe the saltwater from my eyes to clear my vision. The *Endurance* is only 100 yards off. I take a deep breath, go under, and swim for the *Endurance*.

I need to stay beneath the surface to avoid detection. I hold my breath until my lungs burn. The world beneath the ships—the coral reef, the fish, the sea turtles—they go on about their existence. All the animals are unaware of our schemes except a lone dolphin looking at me with its head cocked like a curious puppy.

No time for curious dolphins. I shoo it off and then surface for a quick gasp of air. The *Endurance* is far closer now. I'll reach her hull in one more breath.

I dive.

When I surface again, I touch the slimly wood of the ship's hull, broken only by the colonies of barnacles. I need to climb aboard from the other side—the port side. It isn't facing the *San Paulo*. Less eyes will be watching. The only way to get there is swim directly under the *Endurance*.

I take a deep breath and dive.

I don't know how deep their boat sits so I have to guess. After almost a minute of swimming, I'm sure I've gone deep and far enough. I gently swim up, but the coarse barnacles of the ship's underbelly nip my back. Warm blood flows into the water.

Sharks like blood.

I try to surface again, but I scratch the hull of the ship. How much further could it be? My lungs burn. I'm nearing the end of this breath.

Unable to stay under any longer, I swim up, desperately searching for air. Nothing stops me. I gasp when I break the surface.

Water slides down my face. I wipe my eyes. I'm on the side of the *Endurance* opposite to the *San Paulo*.

I swim silently to the edge of the ship. I find the ladder leading up from the water. The handles are slick. I have to dig my fingernails into the waterlogged wood to keep my grip. I avoid the cannon hatches as I climb, just in case one of them opens. The higher I climb, the less slippery my handholds are. Finally, I reach the railing.

The British sailors move about the deck. Their clean white shirts are tucked into their trousers. All of them look toward the approaching pirate flag. None of them see me as I climb over the railing. I scale the netting leading up to the crow's nest.

If it weren't for the distraction of the *San Paulo*, I would've never managed this. I would've been spotted on my ascent. But no one—not even the lookout—thought to watch their back.

The lookout only notices me when I put my knife to his throat. I say, "If you're quiet, I won't kill you."

I probably couldn't kill him even if he spoke, but I don't tell him that. His eyes nervously dart between me and the approaching pirate ship.

Reluctantly, he hands me his whistle and sets down his rifle. I tear a bit of wet cloth from my pant's leg and stuff it in his mouth. With the rope I carried over my shoulder, I gag him. I use the rest to tie him to the mast. I pull the rope, secure him with a knot, and then pat his cheek. "Sorry about this."

Now I wait for the *Endurance* to deliver the treasure. I won't be able to slip off until the treasure is secured. I sit down next to the lookout to watch.

The *Endurance* slows as it comes to the *San Paulo*. I feel the lost momentum in the crow's nest. The *San Paulo* sits several feet higher in the water than the *Endurance*—hopefully that will change when we load her with treasure. For now, all the *Endurance*'s crew sees are the rifles leaned against the railing and the imposing figure of Gunther, whom they believe is Captain Rodriguez de Medina.

He looks convincing. Even if you had him and Rodriguez standing right next to each other, you wouldn't be able to tell the difference. The real test is not the costume. The real test is how well Gunther plays the role.

The *Endurance*'s crew reach long hooks toward the *San Paulo* to pull her close, so they can lay a plank between the two ships. The usual procedure for surrender. But Gunther shouts, "that's enough. You'll be coming no closer today."

My father, Admiral Higgins steps from beneath the sails where I couldn't see him. One of his hands rests on the railing. The other is wrapped around his officer's saber.

He stands tall. He's an intimidating figure. His hair is well kept, but he has grown a neat beard since I last saw him. Every piece of his British Admiral's uniform is intact despite the heat. The bright red coat is adorned with a gorget, tassles, and two epaulettes. The cuffs are white, and his Admirals hat is black. It casts enough shade to hide his intentions.

With a flick of his head, he calls off his men. He says, "As you wish, Captain Rodriguez."

From my vantage point, I see Charlie crouched below the *San Paulo*'s railing, where the *Endurance*'s crew can't see him. He presses a pistol to Gunther's stomach to ensure he plays his part well.

"Why did you drop your front sail, Captain? We saw it flutter when we surrendered." My father asks a good question. It shows his strength, even in the midst of surrender. Few others would dare question Rodriguez.

Gunther doesn't respond at first. He hadn't been expecting to engage in trivialities. He had planned to demand the treasure and be off.

Gunther strokes his fake beard, as if in deep thought. Charlie presses the pistol deeper into Gunther's stomach.

"Captain?" My father says.

"I am thinking!" Gunther realizes his mistake and frantically shakes his head.

Think fast, Gunther. We're all dead if you don't.

"We're going to buy a new one when we come to port. Had holes in it, it did." He forgets his accent and slips into his English vernacular.

"It looked fine to me." My father squints, suspicious of the story he's being fed, and why Captain Rodriguez—a Spaniard—broke into an English accent. Perhaps my father took it as an insult, that Rodriguez was mocking him. Or he has found a chink in our carefully laid plan and is about to slide his dagger in to see what's behind the façade.

"We Spaniards have higher standards than Englishmen." Gunther goes back to his rubbish Spanish accent, trying to regain ground, hoping my father didn't notice his slip. "The sail had holes. Correct men?" Gunther turns to his imaginary crew hiding behind the railing.

Charlie shouts out, "Sí, señor. El sail have mucho holes."

I would have never thought it possible, but Charlie's accent is worse than Gunther's.

My father grunts, unconvinced, but softens his tone and shifts the conversation. "Captain, before we discuss our surrender, may I ask you something else? It's a personal matter. I have reports that you have in your possession a young man of mixed blood. I was told he tried to rob you in Nassau. I have reason to believe he is my son. Do you still have him aboard your ship?"

He's asking for me.

How could he have known I tried to rob Rodriguez? My father is well connected, but for news of the pirate world to reach his ears, he must have very good informants.

My father continues, "If you have him aboard, I am willing to pay any sum you demand for his safe return."

Gunther is silent, unsure what to say.

Such irony. Isabelle, Charlie, and Gunther could easily ransom me now that I'm aboard the *Endurance*.

Gunther has a clever moment and says, "Ah, I remember now. James. I no longer have him. He escaped while we were docked near Havana."

My father perks up at the mention of my name. I let out a deep breath, thankful for Gunther's loyalty. His answer was clever. Not only does it dissuade my father, he'll head straight to Havana to look for me. It'll discourage him from trying to follow us.

"Thank you, Captain," my father says earnestly. "What are your demands?"

"All the treasure in your hold. We know you are carrying a quarter ton. We expect it all."

"Let us make plank with you. You can come take it yourself." Thankful for news of me as he may be, he senses something amiss. He's testing Gunther, pushing this to go anyway but how he wants it to. This is a classic power move. Force your opponent to play by your rules.

That is what our plan attempted to do to my father. But now he is playing a reversal. Thankfully, Gunther is able to parry.

"Not today, Admiral. I have decided to do things differently. You'll be delivering the gold to that island over there." Gunther points to the smallest of the islands in the distance. "Once you deposit the treasure, you will leave. Quickly, before I change my mind on sparing your lives."

"Very well, give me one moment, Captain." My father turns from the *San Paulo* to his own men and speaks in a subdued voice. "Beckham, report."

No one among the crew answers.

"Beckham. Are you listening?" He looks toward the crow's nest.

No one answers. The lookout squirms and mumbles. He must be Beckham. I quickly speak in his place. "Aye, Admiral."

In a voice soft voice my father asks, "How many men are aboard the *San Paulo*?"

He definitely knows something isn't right. He can't describe what it is, but something strange is happening. From the dropped sails to the terrible Spanish accents, he senses an odd bluff in a game he doesn't know the rules to. But my father is quick to learn and even quicker to win.

"More men than I can count, sir, all armed to the teeth," I lie.

"I see," my father says. I wonder if he recognized my voice because he's silent for a moment. He turns from the crow's nest and says quietly, "Men, prepare to board the *San Paulo*."

"Admiral, of our demands?" Gunther yells.

"One moment, Captain. I'm having my men locate the cargo manifest." He nods to his first mate. "Get the keys to the rifle box."

I jerk the blue cloth from my pocket. I wave it in the air where Charlie can see. Charlie catches sight of it, acknowledges, and scurries to the gun deck hatch. He'll pass word to Isabelle. She'll know what to do.

The sailors arm themselves with the speed and order the British navy is known for. Before Gunther realizes what's happening, they form lines along the railing, ready to attack. Two crewmen reach out with long hooks to pull in the *San Paulo*.

Gunther holds up his hands as to surrender when the hammers cock back. But Charlie runs back to Gunther. He digs his pistol into his side. I can't hear his words, but I see Charlie whisper, *"Dance, monkey."*

Gunther lowers his arms and stutters, "Admiral Higgins, cease and desist! You'll stop your absurd actions. Deliver the treasure now, or I'll—I'll—" The cannon hatches swing open beneath him. He starts but quickly realizes his opportunity and says, "or I'll blow you out of the water! Then I'll come back with a diving bell to fish the treasure out later."

Even my father staggers back when the hatches chink open, revealing the cannons. The men under his command look to each other, unsure what to do. Unsure whether they're about to die or not. They're ready to jump ship to avoid the coming volley.

My father lowers his head, defeated. At this range, the *San Paulo* would decimate the *Endurance*. Few would survive the onslaught. This is unacceptable to my father.

"Lay down your arms, men." He turns to Gunther and says, "You'll have your treasure, you bloody pirate."

15

TREASURE

So much gold. From the crow's nest, I listen to the English coins clink in their chests. They're lowered into the jolly boats to be taken to the island. The boats trudge across the sea like fat sea turtles laden with treasure. Part of the gold sits on the pure white sand, ready to be collected. Gold bars, gold coins, jewelry, and jewels glitter in the sun.

The plan is far from complete, but we've done it. The hard part at least. I've deposed a pirate captain, taken his ship, and robbed the largest spoil of English treasure the New World has ever seen. Right from underneath my own father's nose. Even after the treasure is divided four ways, I've won a fortune.

My heart thumps. The last of the chests are set ashore the small island. It has become the single richest island in the Caribbean. Stacks of chests and piles of spilled gold are littered among the seashells. The crew wasn't careful about unloading the treasure. A chest of pearls lays strewn across the sand.

Any moment now, the *Endurance* will begin her journey toward Havana. Then I will depart, never again to see my father.

My father moves about the bridge below me, taking inventory of the treasure he has lost, and making notes to write his report. It will be hard for him to justify how he lost such a fortune. But his military career is distinguished enough that his superiors will understand.

"Is that all of it?" my father asks his first mate.

"Yes, sir." The first mate stands with his arms behind his back.

They look at the *San Paulo*. She's gently rocking in the distance, drifting as if she no longer has an anchor. As soon as the *Endurance* leaves, she'll come collect me and the treasure.

"It makes me sick that they're getting all of this," the first mate says.

"I know."

"So I suppose you'll be wanting to make a stop in Havana?"

"Do you think we'll have time for it on our return to Long Rock?"

"Of course, Admiral. I'll dust off our Spanish flag." The first mate walks off, leaving my father on the bridge of the ship.

"Men," he calls out, "prepare to make sail. We make for Havana, and then return to the Fortress of Long Rock. I'll ensure that none of you are held accountable for the loss of this treasure. I will bear full responsibility for its capture."

The men are solemn as they move about the ship. They pull anchor. They climb the rigging to drop reefed sails. Soon, they'll climb my mast and find me and Mr. Beckham.

The man still squirms and wiggles, trying to break free of the ropes, but I tied a tight knot.

I pat his shoulder. "Not much longer. Soon, I'll be off, and they'll cut you free."

The front sail drops, catches the wind, and the ship sluggishly moves. They'll climb my mast next to set loose the sails above my head. Time to go before I'm spotted.

I climb the rigging opposite of the *San Paulo*. Even though she drifts in the distance, the men still watch her, prepared for the eccentric Captain Rodriguez to make a move. Having experienced his oddities firsthand, they're ready for any triviality he might throw.

If only they knew the truth—that Captain Rodriguez is probably still on some deserted beach. That an old drunk and two adolescents are the only ones aboard the *San Paulo*. How much stranger the reality of the situation than anything Captain Rodriguez could have concocted.

My foot slips and I jerk to my right. The rigging flips upside down in a gust of wind. I'm tossed onto my back to the deck of the ship with a thud.

I open my eyes. The blue sky, and every man on the ship, looks down at me. They squint, trying to place my face among the men they know aboard the ship. Instantly they see I am not a British sailor. First, they're confused, but then they realize that I'm a pirate. They don't know how, but they piece together that I was involved. I stole their treasure.

Cutlasses and pistols unsheathe.

If they catch me, my part of the plan is done; my share of the treasure gone.

All I have is the dagger strapped to my leg. I jump to my feet, take note of the thirty British sailors, and then notice the crane line. If you cut that rope, the weight at the other end will zip you high into the masts. From there, I'll walk along the cross beam and jump into the ocean.

The men haven't moved, unsure of what to do, but I'm ready. I rush for the rope. My father looks down from the bridge. His eyes meet mine and I stop.

His face is four years older than I remember. Worry lines crisscross his brow and around his green eyes. Eyes we share. A few scars have been added to his collection, notably one across his nose. Despite the signs of age, my father is well and fit.

His eyes widen. "James…"

After all this time, it must be like seeing a ghost. After all the distance he has crossed seeking me, I came to him.

My father and I shared one interest—books. He also read about great men and the writings of the wise. He too believed in fate.

The crew, knowing he has spent years looking for me, await orders.

I take advantage of the lull. I dart for the crane line. I jerk my dagger from its sheath, grab the rope, and cut. My stomach drops. The dagger is ripped from my hand by the force of the upward ascent. I'm lifted to the highest crossbeam in the ship.

Frantically, I wrap my arms around the beam, unable to get a good hold. My fingers find the rope. I find a foothold in the reefed sail. I climb on top of the beam and look down. Dizziness hits me like a wave. I wobble. The deck is as far away from me as earth must be from heaven. Only I'm no angel and I have no wings.

Down below, my father shouts, "James, hang on! Be careful, I'm coming to you."

"Stay where you are, Father!" I say.

He throws off his admiral coat and hands his hat to his first mate. He drops his weapon belt and climbs. He dashes up the rigging as if he were a young man. He's moving quickly, hand over hand, up the netting to my crossbeam.

I scuttle along the beam, straddling it like a horse. Once I'm over water, I'll jump.

I'll need to break the water feet first. It'll keep the air from being knocked from my chest. I'm to the edge of the beam, ready to jump. My father's hand reaches past the topsail rigging. He pulls himself onto the beam with me. He straddles it and says, "James, wait."

I don't wait. I hop from the end of the beam and keep my feet pointed toward the water. As if I hit solid ground, my legs sting. Water swirls around me. I go deep beneath the waves. When I stop diving, I jerk in the water and swim to the surface.

I'm a fair distance from the ship. The evening sun reflects against the surface of the water, obscuring my vision. The world is painted orange. In the distance, a short swim away, is the deserted island laden with treasure.

I make for the island.

Two small splashes crack behind me. A white shirt flutters. My father's boots and shirt.

He jumps from the beam as I did. He splashes behind me. Drops of water lick the back of my head. He breaks the surface, and swims toward me.

My father is a faster swimmer than me. He quickly approaches me from behind. If I hadn't had a head start, I wouldn't have beaten him to the island.

I pull myself onto the sand. My father stands in the shallows behind me. He's got me. I'll be going with him. I won't have my share of the treasure. Isabelle made our creed clear—fall behind get left behind. I look at the piles of treasure I could have had. I sigh.

It was a clever plan and, for the other three conspirators involved, it worked flawlessly. I won't betray them to my father. I'll never tell him that only three people were aboard the *San Paulo*.

Once my father and I leave this island, Gunther, Charlie, and Isabelle will come collect their treasure. They'll only have to split it three ways.

The sand on the beach is warm. The distant sun is a gentle orange. It's low enough that you can watch it sink into the sea. I sit down, facing the sun, my lost treasure to my back. Seashells litter the beach. Hermit crabs scuttle across the sand. I pick one up and dig a small hole in the sand for its cage.

Soon I will have my own cage.

One way or another. A prison cell when I am charged with piracy, or my father's house in Barbados.

My father walks from the surf, dripping with sea water. He sits down next to me without a word. He wrings the water from his hair and looks toward the sun. We're quiet as it lowers beneath the waves.

It's hard to know what to say after four years. Even in normal conversation, words are treacherous, not to be trusted. They misrepresent what you mean and what you actually want to say.

Sitting in silence next to my father as the sun sets feels natural—like something we should have done a long time ago and done often. Fathers and sons don't bond over words or feelings or by way of lessons; they bond through shared experiences.

I'm strangely content with this moment. I don't think about running or what comes next. My ill feelings toward my father feel far away.

The last sliver on the sun sinks below the waves. Only then does my father turn to me and say, "I've missed you, James."

My emotions overflow. "I missed you too, Father."

———

Four years ago, when I was twelve, I ran away from home. Rain pounded the roof of our home in Barbados. I couldn't sleep that night. Too many changes were happening far too quickly. Too much uncertainty.

I was laying in my bed, tossing and turning, mulling over what had happened in the past year. It all began with a wedding.

Before the ceremony, my father said, "There will be a few small changes, but nothing will ever change the fact that you are my son."

"I know, Father."

"I want you to stand among my groomsmen at the wedding."

"I will, Father," I said.

My father married an English woman named Emily. She was the daughter of a puritan pastor. My father was a staunch Anglican. Emily's father made an exception. He allowed my heathen father, a promising Captain, to marry his puritan daughter.

I was proud to be standing by his best man—his first mate of many years. The wedding was simple. Puritan style. The church was devoid of decoration, but even the puritans make allowance for a white arch with greenery for the couple to stand beneath.

My father stood with Emily's maid of honor beneath the arch, waiting for the bride.

She came walking down the aisle in a white lace dress. Even beneath the veil you could see bright blue eyes, brighter than the sea at midday. After looking at my father for a long time, she glanced at me and smiled. She took her place in the front of the church.

Her father, the puritan pastor, presided over the ceremony.

Though my father promised little would change, a year later, everything was changing.

My father and I lived alone before the wedding. Our home reflected this. Despite the best efforts of my nanny, clothes, books, guns, toy soldiers, empty glasses, and bowls littered the house. He and I lived the way we liked, made messes without cleaning them up, and ate food in the parlor. We took milk to bed. Now, the ordering of our home was different. Now, I shared my house with a stranger who tried to be my mother.

The home was kept clean, like a church. All the meals had to be eaten in the dining room. No food or drink was allowed in the parlor and certainly not in the bedrooms. I had to clean up my books and anything else I happened to be working on. I could no longer leave my papers strewn across the floor.

This was a hard change for my father as well. He too liked to spread out his papers, books, and navigation charts across the house. The mess, he said, helped him think, but he gave in to Emily's desire for an orderly home.

"An orderly home is a sign of an orderly life," she often told my father.

"Yes, dear."

She was kind. She took good care of my father and me. Though I was a mark of my father's past indiscretions, she didn't treat me as a secret to be hidden. I was living proof that my father had been with other women. Yet she smiled at me when I passed her in the hallway, or while she made me dinner.

On the night I ran away, she had been living with us for a year. I heard a knock on my bedroom door. I took the candle burning next to my bed and walked to the door. It creaked open. My step-mother stood outside. She seemed tired. I often heard crying in the night followed by her footsteps. Her brown hair was pulled into a messy bun. Her nightgown flowed in long plats like an angel.

She stepped into my room. "You know all of this changes nothing. You can come out of your room if you want."

What happened last week while my father was at sea changed everything.

"You know that I think of you as my son. You can call me mother, if you like, but I will never force you. You're a part of this family." She touched my shoulder. "You were here before me and you'll always be here. The three of us will keep each other company while your father is at sea." A gentle smile spread across her face despite the silence between us. "You can trust me, James. Your father is downstairs if you want to see him. He just arrived."

She squeezed my shoulder as she walked out of my room.

I crept to the parlor of our home. The walls were painted light blue and the wood carving along the ceiling was ornate. Paintings of ships lined the wall. I peered in the door. My father couldn't see me watching.

A fire crackled in the fireplace. The thunder rumbled outside, splashing blue light into the room. My father softly sang to the bundle in his arms—his legitimate born son.

16

<hr>

THE FORTRESS OF LONG ROCK

MY FATHER AND I SIT ON THE SHORE OF THE TREASURE LADEN island for a long time. The stars come out, clear as lanterns, and my father senses we've been here long enough. He waves for his men to send a boat to ferry us to the *Endurance*.

As the boat approaches, my father asks, "Where've you been, James?"

"I jumped from port to port. You'd be proud of me. Before now, I did honest work. I never stole, except when I tried to steal from Captain Rodriguez before my capture."

"I knew you would do the best you could. I worried, but not too much. I knew you were resourceful. I also knew that one day I would find you. Or you would, as it seems, find me. Fate works that way, doesn't it?"

I look back at the treasure before answering. "Yeah."

"I know it's hard to see what would have been your share of that go."

If only he knew how large my share would have been.

He pats me on the shoulder but doesn't say anything else. The jolly boat beaches. The men help us board. Then they row us to the ship.

Aboard the *Endurance*, the men ignore me. My father didn't explain how I was involved with stealing the treasure. However, from the testimony of Beckham—the lookout I tied up—the crew gathered that I am a pirate.

Another black mark on my father's record. He must be well respected to have been made Admiral. Now he's lost the greatest treasure in the New World. How long can he remain an Admiral with that record? Not only does he have an illegitimate son, his illegitimate son is a criminal.

My actions, as much as my existence, will hinder his ambitions.

Still, the crew, out of respect for my father, left me be. They satisfy themselves with casting me cold, condescending looks.

The men move about their work, lifting sails, pulling ropes, scrubbing the deck, jabbering. The *Endurance* sails smoother than the *San Paulo*. Not only is she fully manned, she's a well-made ship. The *San Paulo* hobbled—an ugly beast gutted and remade for our purposes. The *Endurance* moves like an animal born of the sea.

Charlie, Gunther, and Isabelle are probably celebrating as they haul the treasure aboard the *San Paulo*. They're sifting through the gold and spending it in their minds. I expect Charlie's got a ring on each finger, a gold pendant around his neck, and a crown on his head. Gunther's probably smiling. Isabelle is counting her share and glancing toward the horizon, deciding where she'll go next.

Thinking about Isabelle hurts the most. She sashays about my mind in her men's clothes. Her black hair blown by the sea breeze. I can only think about what could have been. The four of us, living in Africa. Each of us happy with the treasure we'd daringly won. Now it's just the three of them. I wouldn't be surprised if they ventured separate ways.

Some things can't be fixed or made straight. They can't be patched, repaired, or changed. They are simply, irreversibly broken.

It was a clever plan. I played the game and I lost. It's time for what comes next.

My father gave me dry clothes, a mismatch of brown pants and a naval shirt—some of his own. They're baggy and flutter with each gust of wind.

We're sailing to—I'm not sure exactly where we're sailing. But the *Endurance* moves with fierce determination to reach wherever her destination may be.

My father stands on the bridge of the ship, looking across the night, lost deep in thought. He must be trying to figure a way to explain the loss of the treasure.

I feel guilty about the position I've put him in. I hadn't considered what my actions would cost him. Now I see his worry and his loss.

I climb the stairs to the bridge of the *Endurance*. I stand beside him.

"Where are we going?" I ask.

"The Fortress of Long Rock."

Long Rock is the smallest British fortress in the Caribbean. It's situated on a small island in the Florida Keys, deep in Spanish territory. It was intended to be a rally point in war. However, it's too remote to keep well stocked. From what I've heard, it's little more than a pile of stones with a few canons on top. It's the fortress from where Captain Solway of the *London Wolf* sails.

"Why are we going there?"

"I need to dock and write my report about the loss of the *Endurance's* treasure. Then send it to His Majesty in England."

"Aren't we closer to the Fortress at Key Largo?" I remember seeing all the British forts marked on the map. I made mental notes as Charlie plotted our intercept with the *Endurance*.

"You're right. Key Largo also has a better bay for anchor. But I have reason for going to Long Rock."

"Why?"

"Long Rock is under my command. If we made anchor at Key Largo, I would have no say what happened to you. James, you're wanted on counts of piracy now."

My heart drops. Piracy is a capital crime. I knew when I stole the *San Paulo* and made plans to rob the *Endurance* that I was a pirate. But I hadn't considered the full consequences. I didn't think I would have to. If everything had gone to plan, I would be on my way to Africa.

"But at Long Rock," my father continues, "I can protect you."

"Long Rock, up ahead, Admiral!" Beckham calls down from the crow's nest. He scowls at me before returning his gaze to the horizon.

As we enter the bay, we pass a log strung up in the trees. From that log, hanging by nooses, are four men. Their eyes picked out by the birds, their flesh rotting from their bones. Their clothes hang in rags, soiled by the elements. Above them, written on a wooden sign is, 'Pirates, beware.'

Captain Solway's handiwork.

My father touches my shoulder. I jump.

"James, I won't let that happen to you." He points to the hanged pirates. "I'm not sure what we'll do, but I won't let them hang you there. While we're at Long Rock, you're safe. We'll come up with a plan, make up a story for why you were aboard the *San Paulo*. We'll say you were forced, or better yet, that you were a prisoner I found thrown overboard. The men aboard this ship are loyal to me. They'll tell whatever story I ask them to. I'm sure even Beckham will come around. He's still a bit peeved about being tied up. You might want to apologize to him, smooth things over to ensure he'll keep to whatever story I tell him." My father smiles. "It will all be all right, James. I can still do right by you."

I want to let myself fall into my father's words, to rest there, but the past holds me back. Being abandoned as a child and then replaced by a legitimate heir are my chains. They pull me back from my father's love.

Yet after all I've done, the black marks I've written across his record, my father still wants to help me—to do right by me.

Despite feeling conflicted, I say, "Thank you."

He nods and steps from the bridge to supervise docking the *Endurance* with the fortress. Night has fallen. Bringing a ship to port in the dark is tricky.

The fortress of Long Rock, while considered small, still stands taller than the palm trees. It stands so tall that I have a difficult time imagining men stacking rocks that high. It's like a grey box with watch towers.

Cannons protrude from every opening along the side facing the ocean. A British flag flies from the pole at the top. Long Rock is a safe haven for passing English ships. Even though it's a small fort, it has total control of the bay. Every angle in the bay is within canon sight. This fortress would be impossible to invade.

If a ship were being chased by pirates, it could make for Long Rock and seek refuge. Few would be mad enough to try to attack a ship under the protection of the fortress.

Joining us in the bay is the *London Wolf*—Captain Solway's ship. The ship rests in the bay like a sleeping sea monster. The *London Wolf* is the largest ship that sails this stretch of ocean. Even Spanish galleons shy away when they see the Man of War approach. All three of her masts are reefed and her anchor is dropped.

The *Endurance* comes to port alongside the rickety timber pier.

Captain Solway walks onto the dock. He must have been in the fortress and seen the *Endurance* approaching. He's carrying a lantern and wearing a nightgown. He acts surprised to see the *Endurance*.

I remember his face. Charlie and I bumped into him last night after stealing the *San Paulo*. In the lantern light, more details are revealed. He's several years older than my father. His grey hair is kept in a neat pony tail. His eyes are dark—like a shark's. Even though my father is several years younger, he outranks the Captain.

"Admiral Higgins," Captain Solway says "is everything alright? My orders state that you were bound for England."

"Good evening, Captain. We've had an incident," my father says.

"What's happened? It wasn't pirates was it? I passed a suspicious ship last night. I regret not searching them. They claimed to be goat traders, but they stank of pirates."

I duck my head and hope Captain Solway doesn't recognize me.

"I'm afraid it was pirates. There's nothing you could have done. It was Rodriguez de Medina who took the fortune. I need to write my report to send to His Majesty."

"They should have let me accompany you! I protested, you know I did, but His Majesty insisted that I keep watch over Long Rock and the surrounding ocean. Even Rodriguez de Medina would've thought twice about robbing you if he had seen the *London Wolf* at your side. I suppose none of it matters now though. I'll have your study prepared. Who is this?" The captain points to me.

"A boy cast over by the *San Paulo's* crew."

"A pirate? Is he your prisoner?"

"No, I believe he was held as a prisoner aboard the *San Paulo*. I don't know why or to what end. I intend to question him and see if we can deduce the *San Paulo's* next port of call. Maybe we can take back the treasure." My father lies.

Perhaps Commander Solway senses this. After killing so many pirates, maybe he can recognize the look in their eyes. Or perhaps he learned to see the make of their souls. He squints at me. "Very well, I will prepare guest chambers."

"No, he will be staying with me."

"As you wish, Admiral."

I follow my father and Captain Solway through the heavy doors of the fortress. They close behind us.

Beckham passes us. He intentionally bumps my shoulder, then leers at me. He walks ahead and talks to Captain Solway. The two whisper and disappear down the hall.

My father and I climb the spiral stairs into the heights of the fortress. I pause by the window to take one last breath of fresh air. It'll be a long night confined in the fortress.

A ship, flying British colors, sits far from the fortress, beyond the range of the canons. Why don't they enter into port if they're a friend? It's as if the ship is trying to make up its mind whether or not to venture in. I shrug my shoulders. Captains are an odd sort. Perhaps being near the fortress is enough to make this ship feel safe.

Odd, but I leave the window and follow my father to his study.

17

THE WAY THE WORLD IS

My father stands taut, arms crossed behind his back as he looks out the glassless window. Antiquated shelves line all the walls but one. That wall is home to a crackling fire, two cushy chairs, and a table set with wine. My father stays by the window. He watches the ship I saw earlier come into the bay. It seems they finally made the decision to come in.

He takes off his Admiral's coat and hat. He hangs them on a hook. He kicks off his boots. Then, with a deep sigh, he slides into a chair by the fire. He reaches to pour a glass of wine. After hesitating, he pours a second and offers it to me.

"You're old enough for this now."

I take the glass and sit in the chair opposite of my father.

"James, why did you run away?"

An uncharacteristic anger, like a monster living inside me I'd never noticed, wakes. I stand up, accidentally knocking over the glass of wine. "Because you were never home." I start to cry. "Because you were always away with Governor Cardoso. Because you abandoned my mother after I was born. Because you replaced me with my half-brother!"

My father stands too, but gently. Pain creases the lines of his worn face. Yet another emotion lies beneath. Even as I curse him, he looks on me with love.

Without a word, he hugs me.

He hadn't hugged me since I was little. My head slumps onto his shoulder.

He gently eases me toward my chair and sits me back down. As he watches the fire he says, "James, would you like to know everything?"

I wipe the tears from my eyes, embarrassed of them. I steady myself. Men don't act this way. Yet my father doesn't react to what I consider weakness. I had forgotten one of his most gracious traits. He is not judging or cruel. He is hard—yes—but he is also kind. He understands that even the strongest men break.

"Yes, I want to know," I say.

He pours me another glass of wine. "Can we begin with your mother?"

"Yes."

"I expect you heard rumors as you were growing up?"

"Many."

"The relationship wasn't as they said. I can promise you that. She was a slave on a tobacco plantation in Charleston. Her name was Jasmine."

My father stops and looks toward the floor.

I'd never known her name. The name fits the image I held of her—a slender black woman, clothed in sackcloth. A woman with a narrow face. Jasmine. It's a gentle name.

"I was stationed there to protect the plantation from the natives. It was there I met her. You know how blacks are viewed, James. But I didn't care. She was clever. She had dreams too big for a slave. You've surely learned how these things go."

"You loved her, and she loved you?" I ask.

"Yes, but it was a secret, until she became pregnant with you. I offered her owner a fortune for her freedom, but he was suspicious. He eventually learned my reason for wanting to purchase her. Our coupling was considered grotesque—an abomination. The Church condemned the matching. The magistrate ordered that you be sold into slavery yourself. He said that you were not my son—you were property of Jasmine's owner. I stole you and your mother away in the night. She was caught, but she thrust you into my arms and told me to run. I brought you to the Caribbean, where the world is less civilized. Where it's a little more open to a man having a mixed son."

"You just left her there?" I ask.

"I had to save you. You would have grown up a slave. I went back to look for her, but she had been sold to a different plantation owner. And then that plantation owner sold her. When I finally tracked her down, there was nothing left but a grave."

My father hits the table. "I was angry for a long time, James. Angry that the world is the way it is. She was a far better person than any of her masters." He looks up at me. "So I made a promise. I promised that I would make a place in this world for you."

I sense he doesn't see me anymore. He sees the baby to whom he made an impossible promise.

"Could I end the practice of slavery or make people see blacks as I did? No. But somehow I would make this world better for you than it was for your mother."

Weight lifts off my chest. He didn't willingly abandon her. He was forced because he had to save me. I feel guilty for the ill-feelings I have harbored.

My father leans back in his chair, exhausted by the memories of my mother. And by the stupidity of the world—its brutality—and the practice of treating humans as less than human.

"I was away often. I think that was your other accusation. I'll admit to you that I lost myself in my work. I could have come to port more often than I did. I enjoyed work and spent most of the spare time I had climbing ranks. I hope you can forgive me for—"

"I forgive you," I blurt out. I'm ready to let go of old hurts, to have peace.

"Thank you. But not all my time was spent in duty to the Crown. You mentioned my relationship with the governor of Havana. Our friendship is a long story."

"I want to know."

"Francisco Cardoso and I grew up together before the war started. We both spoke Spanish and English. We didn't realize Spaniards were supposed to dislike the British. Or that the British hated Spaniards. All I knew was that we both liked to play swords with sticks.

"He grew up to be a bit odd, as you probably remember. He inherited a fortune from his family and eventually came to the New World as the Governor of Havana."

I smile when I think of the Governor Francisco Cardoso—the fiery man who told me I was worth something with a mere look. He was the idealist who awoke my character.

"Before I met your mother, long before you were born, Francisco sent word for me. The war between Spain and Great Britain had erupted and casualties were huge. The Spanish held greater power in the Caribbean, and yet the English still fought. Neither would give ground. Francisco sent a note instructing me to visit him in Havana, under the cover of night in a ship bearing the Spanish flag. Because of our childhood friendship, I did as he requested. He told me he believed there could be a peace. He said the two kingdoms didn't have to fight, at least not in the New World.

"He had a plan to secretly broker a peace between the British and Spanish colonies. It was a mutual agreement to stop the needless conflict in the Caribbean, even if the war raged in Europe.

"I told him he was mad. The world is what it is. We were friends, but the British and Spaniards, and all the other kingdoms of this world, would always fight. It was just the way things were. I left and didn't think of him again for many years.

"After your mother was ripped from me, I contacted Francisco once more. I had a promise to keep. And he was the only one who might help me keep it. He'd gone loopy by that time. His plan for peace was as outrageous as it was ambitious. However, he believed that with the help of a British captain, his secret plan could come to pass.

"I knew I could never end the practice of slavery. I knew that in 'civilized' places you would always be seen as less than human. I did my best to protect you from that. Even if I couldn't change that, I could at least end the war threatening your future livelihood in the New World.

"But James, my time with Francisco taught me that the world doesn't have to be the way it is. The wars, the strife, the hate. It's all created by us.

The world can be changed by men who are clever enough to fix it. Francisco and I are almost there. A treaty was recently signed."

I didn't catch everything he said about the world being changeable. Or what he meant about the end of the British and Spanish war. But I believe him.

All he did, he did for me.

"I married Emily when you got older. I refrained from marrying for a long time, but Emily was good for me. You were never going to be replaced. Emily and I agreed that you would always be a part of our family. You have a new baby sister now, by the way."

"Thank you, Father. For all of it."

My father smiles as if that 'thank you' was all he had wanted for many years. "Of course, James."

The fire crackles. I breathe deep and exhale easily. I'm at peace with my father. I'm as peaceful as Isabelle was the night we spoke about Sophocles on the deck of the *San Paulo*.

One treasure lost, another won.

"Every man has to make his own way in the world. I've done my best for you. You can come back to Barbados with me. You'll always have a place under my roof, but I don't expect you to do that. You're not my prisoner and I can't control you. I'm not sure what you'll do, but you'll make your own way. And I'll be proud of you for it." My father pauses. "I just hope you won't continue to keep the company of pirates."

"I won't."

"Thank you, son. Are you hungry?"

I hadn't realized it, but at the word 'hungry' my stomach growls. "Yes."

"I'll go find us some dinner. I'll be back in a few minutes. I'm sure the cook keeps a thing or two stashed in the kitchen."

He walks out of the study.

I lean back in my chair, considering all he told me. It had to have all been true. It explains everything—the midnight visits with the Governor, the time he spent away from home, the reason he couldn't save my mother.

I stand up, walk about the room, and stretch. Outside the window, the ship coming into the bay turns herself around before stopping. She faces the mouth of the bay, as if she's ready to run.

The door to the study is closed. I test the lock. The door knob turns, and the door clicks open. My father was telling the truth. I'm no prisoner here. I feel guilty for having tested the door.

I sit down and await my father. He'll be back soon and we'll—

The door swings open. Captain Solway walks in with Beckham. Solway stands tall—self-righteous—and he holds an official, wax stamped parchment in his hand. A malicious grin spreads across his face. "You're a pirate."

I stand up and back toward the window. I look down to the beach below. The wind tugs at my shirt, inviting me to jump, to make my escape, but it's a thirty-foot drop. I'd never make it unscathed.

Beckham must have told him what happened when the *Endurance* was robbed. He told Captain Solway of my involvement.

Captain Solway points a pistol toward my chest. "Don't run, boy. You'll be hanged tomorrow. But tonight, you'll be held in the dungeon. Take him below."

At his order, several red coat soldiers spill through the door and shackle my wrists. The cold iron is heavy. It scratches at my skin. By a chain, they yank me to the cells buried beneath the fortress.

———

The walls of my cell are made of cold stones. My only light is the moon coming through the barred window near the ceiling. Silence tells me that I'm the only prisoner. I pace the cell, looking for a weakness. The stones are solidly mortared, the window is too high, and the door is latched tight.

I sit down in the corner. I'm instantly soaked by the puddles on the floor.

I thought my defeat was complete when I was captured by my father. However, he showed me how I could manage a fresh start.

No fresh start now though. Tomorrow I'll hang.

No, I won't.

My father will save me from this. He outranks Solway. He can give the order to release me.

Even if my father isn't able to save me, I'm Captain James Higgins of the *San Paulo*. The brilliant lad who stole a ship from the most feared pirate in the Caribbean. If I can steal a ship, surely I can sneak out of this fortress.

The thick, iron door to my cell crashes open in an explosion. Knocked off its hinges, it tumbles to the stone floor with a metallic clunk.

My ears ring. I stagger back. Charlie bolts in. He's got a crazed look in his eyes and a pistol in each hand. His face is painted black and his clothes are smeared with charcoal to blend with the night. A bandolier of hand bombs is strung over his shoulder. He surveys the room, making a wide arch with his two guns before tipping his head toward the door.

Isabelle walks in, her hair in a tight ponytail. A black bandana is wrapped around her head. She, too, is heavily armed. She has both cutlasses drawn as she enters the room.

She grabs me by the arm, pulls me to my feet, and says, "We're rescuing you."

18

BELLUM ROMANUM

Isabelle checks behind her for the soldiers she expects to storm the dungeon. Explosions don't tend to go unnoticed. Charlie and Isabelle are grizzled, their movements are quick, and their actions were carefully planned.

"Gunther has the *San Paulo* in the bay and is ready to run. Are you coming or not?" Isabelle snaps. She looks back at me, wondering why I haven't followed her out of the cell.

Charlie and Gunther might have come after me, but they wouldn't have faced a British fortress. But Isabelle—she had no reason at all. She had the right to leave me to the British. Yet I'm sure she was the architect of my rescue.

"Why?" I ask.

Her shoulders loosen. She faces me. *"Go then, if you must, but remember, no matter how foolish your deeds, those who love you will still love you,"* she quotes her favorite passage from Antigone. "The four of us are in this together. Take this." She hands me a cutlass.

We move uninterrupted through the maze of stone passageways. Charlie walks up ahead, carrying a torch that colors the stone walls a dancing orange. I squint my eyes to see in the dim light.

The stairs at the end of the tunnel lead to the main level of the fortress.

"Hold this." Charlie hands Isabelle the torch. He creeps up the stairs and pokes his nose out the door. "It's chaos up there. They can't figure out where the explosion came from. Two soldiers are heading our way. Put the torch out, quick. Get down."

Charlie jumps the stairs in one leap. He huddles with Isabelle and I in a broom closet beneath. The three of us cram in together.

"Charlie, what's the plan?" Isabelle asks.

"You told me to get us into the fort. You didn't tell me to have a plan for getting us out."

"That should have gone without saying," Isabelle whispers, angrily. "So, you have no plan for how to get out? You expected us to just walk through the gates?"

"No, I—"

The door to the dungeons opens. Light from the fortress above spills in. Boots click down the stairs slowly—as if they're anticipating another explosion.

Charlie looks out a crack in the closet door.

"How many?" I ask.

"Only two," Charlie says.

Thoughts tumble in my mind as I develop a plan for our escape. The two soldiers search the room. It won't take them long to find us. But I have an idea. This is a fortress. Only one tactic can be effectively employed.

"*Bellum Romanum*," I say.

Isabelle grins dangerously. *"War as the Romans did it."*

Bellum Romanum—the full, savage, indiscriminate force of the Roman Empire. This is the war we will wage on Captain Solway.

"We'll take out the two soldiers and steal their uniforms," I whisper. "The two of you will wear the uniforms. I will act as the prisoner. As we move through the fortress, Charlie will set off more hand bombs. Then in the chaos, we make our escape."

Isabelle draws her cutlass. "Charlie, you hit the guy on the left and I'll handle the one on the right."

Charlie takes a hand bomb. The bombs are shaped like cannon balls and are nearly as heavy.

The closet door creaks open. Charlie and Isabelle rush out. Charlie bludgeons the first soldier with the bomb, knocking him to the floor. The soldier doesn't move. He's either out cold or dead.

The second soldier turns around when he hears his friend hit the floor. Isabelle slashes at him with her cutlass. He deflects with his torch. He kicks Isabelle back against the hard stone wall. It knocks the breath from her chest. She slumps to her knees.

The soldier rushes up the stairs, trying to escape to the main level of the fortress. He needs reinforcement to contain the devils lurking in the dungeon.

Before he reaches the top, I grab his ankle and yank him to the floor. He hits his head when he falls.

"Take their clothes." Isabelle field strips the first solder. She takes his white cloth pants, black leather shoes, and red coat with white cuffs and buttons. She puts the uniform on over her own clothes. Once dressed, she drags the soldier to the closet.

I help Charlie into the clothes of the other soldier. I fix his collar and brush off his shoulder. He and I lug the soldier to the closet. We tie him up next to the other and close the door.

Isabelle laughs.

"What?" I ask.

"They're going to be really confused when they wake up naked in there."

I take a pair of shackles from the wall and fasten them around my wrists. I'm careful not to click the locks. Charlie and Isabelle, in British soldier uniforms, stand to either side of me. They pretend they're escorting me elsewhere in the fortress.

"Charlie, stand a little straighter. You're already too short to be a soldier," Isabelle says.

Sand crunches beneath our feet as we walk the corridors. I'm praying we don't attract too much attention. No one seems to mind us though. They're in a tizzy over the explosion in the dungeon.

We go up the stairs to the officer chambers. Past the officer's chambers is the courtyard. Then the main gate.

A voice calls from behind us. "You there!" An overzealous private stops us. "Who goes there?" he demands.

I hang my head limply, pretending to be complacent and defeated.

"Captain Solway's orders," Charlie says. "Something went amiss in the dungeon. An explosion of some sort."

Isabelle remains silent. Her voice would give away her disguise.

"Can't have prisoners in a cell with compromised walls. And you, what's your name and rank?" He turns to Isabelle.

Charlie and Isabelle look toward each other and then to me.

"She's—he's a mute, sir," I quickly say.

Charlie slaps me hard, completing the guise of a harsh soldier. "No more outbursts, prisoner!"

"A mute you say?" The private leans in close to examine Isabelle. "Soft skinned and hairless too. Effeminate." He spits and shakes his head disgustedly. "It's amazing what they'll allow into the navy now. Go on you two. Don't keep Captain Solway waiting."

"Aye, sir," Charlie says.

Charlie and Isabelle usher me down the hall.

"Take a left," I whisper. I remember the way to the main gate. We'll pass my father's quarters.

"Sorry about slapping you, James," Charlie whispers as we walk.

"No worries. He was fooled."

The three of us pass the door of my father's study. I stop, and I reach for the door.

"James, what're you doing?" Isabelle whispers.

"This will only take a second."

The door handle turns, still unlocked. I stumble into the dark room and feel around in the faint light. In the far corner, beneath the shelf of books, is my father's writing desk. Papers are scattered across its surface in no apparent order. A quill in a small well of ink sits near the edge.

Charlie and Isabelle tentatively come into the room.

"Whose room is this?" Charlie asks.

"My father's. Admiral William Higgins." No point in keeping secrets now.

Charlie's eyes widen. "You're the Admiral's son? This whole endeavor keeps getting more tangled. Why can't you and Isabelle be simple like

Gunther and me? Why must you have testy relations with powerful people? You know who my parents were? Goat farmers."

Isabelle looks at me. "Your father and my father were friends." Isabelle rummages through the books lining the wall. She picks a copy of *Antigone* from the shelf. "Admiral Higgins read this to me on his visits." She stuffs the book in her coat.

A clean piece of paper rests at the top of the drawer. I run my finger along its dry surface. I dip the quill. When I finish writing, I fold the paper and leave it among the others competing for desk space.

"Okay let's go," I say.

"That's all? We're visiting the room of a powerful Admiral and all we're stealing is a lousy book and leaving a note?" Charlie says. "Are you two ready to go? Or are you going to tell me you're related to the king of Spain?"

———

Our way through the fortress is unobstructed. A few soldiers give us odd looks as we pass. Charlie hides the bombs beneath his coat. So, the soldiers pay us no mind. They have more pressing issues. We move along the corridors. Charlie discreetly lights, and then tosses hand bombs into random rooms.

The explosions turn the fortress into a madhouse. Men are running about, putting out fires. A mason, with his leather apron put on over his nightgown, is ushered from room to room. He's inspecting the structural integrity of the rooms. Another of Charlie's bombs explode and they rush the mason to that room. The soldiers can't find where the bombs are coming from. All the mason can figure is that the devil came to Long Rock.

With the help of the disguises—and the chaos—we arrive at the main entry gate.

Charlie darts ahead to open the gate, but it doesn't budge. I check over my shoulder to ensure no one is watching and I join him. The gate is sealed shut and we can't force it open.

"We'll use one of the cannons to blast our way out," Isabelle says.

Clever, Isabelle. In a single stroke we'll open the door and render a

British fortress impotent.

Bellum Romanum.

Charlie and I dart for the ladder to the cannons. They're pointed toward the bay, ready to fire on enemy ships. Soon, one will fire on the fortress door. As I put my fingers around the ladder, a voice calls from behind me. "Where are you going?"

Captain Solway steps into the dim moonlight. He's still dressed in a nightgown. When I turn around, he recognizes me. "Men, the prisoner is escaping!"

Charlie climbs the ladder toward the cannons. He's pretending he didn't hear the order.

Isabelle—still in her British soldier uniform—salutes the commander and pulls out her pistol. She aims it at me and cocks the trigger. Her back turned to Solway, she winks at me.

"In the name of the King," Solway begins. Soldiers are running all around him, trying to clear rubble from Charlie's bombs. "I condemn you, James Higgins, to death on counts of piracy on the high seas. Do you have any last words?"

"You would condemn a man to death without trial?" I glance toward Charlie as he uses the ramrod to load a cannon ball.

He needs time.

"By order of the King, men condemned of piracy are granted no trial. Your last words?"

Charlie struggles, but he swivels the cannon toward the door, sticks in the fuse, and gives me a thumbs up.

Isabelle flexes her fingers around the pistol she has pointed at me.

"Your last words?" Captain Solway demands.

I smile.

"Fire!" I yell.

Isabelle swirls around. She fires her pistol at Captain Solway. The bullet catches him in the shoulder and he staggers back. He holds the wound with his other hand. Charlie fires the cannon. It blasts the door, and the stone archway above it, to smithereens.

In the blast, the commander is knocked to the ground. He doesn't move, and I don't check on him. It would be best if he's dead. If he survives, he could give testimony against my father for harboring a pirate.

He doesn't look to be breathing; his chest is still, and his leg is contorted. I pull out my blade to do the deed—for my father—just to be safe. But I stop. No sense in that sort of savagery.

"Come on, James," Charlie shouts as he climbs down the ladder.

We scamper over the ruble where the fortress door once stood. Our feet dig into the soft sand. We run across the beach to the jolly boat hidden in the island's dark shadows.

As they run, Charlie and Isabelle throw off their disguises. A red coat flashes in the moonlight as it flutters to the ground. Then a pair of black boots zip past my head.

I feel the way I did on the night we stole the *San Paulo*. Liberated. I laugh at the sound of the waves. The breath coming out of my lungs feels uninhibited. The fortress is in chaos behind us. Men are shouting, still trying to figure what caused the explosions.

Gunther was right about the three of us.

We're devils, crafty and destructive. Mischievous and mad.

Charlie flips the jolly boat and walks it into the surf. Isabelle and I jump in as it bobbles into the dark ocean. Isabelle and I each take an oar and row away from the decimated British fortress.

The *San Paulo* gently rocks in the distance, flying a friendly British flag. Isabelle and I row the jolly boat to the starboard side. Gunther throws a rope that hits the deck like a coiled snake.

"Took you three a right long time, didn't it?" Gunther calls down.

"How long would it have taken you, fat man?" Charlie says in his usual tit for tat with Gunther.

I hand Isabelle the rope. "You first."

She and then Charlie climb the rope to board the *San Paulo*.

When I look back, I see the fortress and think about my father. He must have been held up in the galley when he went to find us dinner—held up by Captain Solway's men, perhaps. I hope he got out okay. Of course he got out okay. He's Admiral William Higgins. He'll regain control of the fortress.

Gunther wiggles the rope, telling me it's time to climb aboard the *San Paulo*. The rope is rough in my hands. It scratches my fingers. I shimmy up the hull of my ship. I approach the railing, and Gunther grabs my hand and pulls me over. "Good to have you back aboard, Captain."

19

ESCAPE FROM LONG ROCK

THE SHIP IS QUIET. SHE SWAYS WITH THE EBB AND FLOW OF THE bay. The three ships—the *San Paulo*, the *Endurance*, and the *London Wolf* float as if they're unaware of the chaotic fortress. I allow myself a deep breath. Smoke pricks my nose and makes it raw. We should leave now, but I watch our handiwork—the fortress fires that soldiers are rushing to put out, the *San Paulo*, the treasure.

The treasure! My mind snaps to glittering piles of treasure on a deserted island. The gold resting on the sand beneath the setting sun. I ask, "Did you get the treasure?"

"No, we loved you so much we dropped everything and ran after the *Endurance*." Charlie cups his hands under his chin and bats his eye lashes. "Of course we got the bloody treasure. We loaded it up before we followed the *Endurance*. Once we're to sea, you'll have to go take a look. It really sparkles."

"Thank you." My gaze moves between the three members of my crew. Gunther, Charlie, and Isabelle stand at the bridge of the ship. Charlie wipes the soot from his face and throws his old shirt to the sea before putting on a fresh one. Isabelle stands by the wheel. Gunther watches the fortress.

"What are your orders, Captain?" Charlie asks.

I smile because I realize that our journey is done. The four of us have won. "To sea and then plot us a course straight for Africa!" My three-member crew cheers. Isabelle and Charlie wave their cutlasses high in the air.

Charlie dashes to the railing of the bridge. He pulls a rope strung to the front sail. Several small bands of rope fall from the mast. The sail flaps as it catches wind. Charlie's work is impressive.

A voice from the fortress, carried by the wind, rings across the bay, "It's the *San Paulo*! The *San Paulo* is anchored in the bay! Prepare the cannons to fire!"

Gunther cranes toward the sound of the voice.

"And by God, there's Captain Rodriguez himself! Fire! Fire! Fire!" The soldier shouting must have seen Gunther disguised earlier today and now believes him to be Rodriguez.

A cannon fires. The ball splashes into the ocean off the stern of the *San Paulo*.

Apparently, the fortress isn't in the disarray I imagined it to be. The entry gate is in shambles, but the fortress walls, and their rows of cannons, are intact. Isabelle hands me a spyglass.

Commander Solway doggedly climbs the stone stairs to the top of the wall. He holds his side as he staggers about the cannons, ordering them to all be fired.

"Sink her! She has the king's treasure aboard! We'll fish it from the bay after she's sunk." Commander Solway waves his arms, the signal for all the cannons to fire.

The cannons blast, each shot landing closer and closer to its mark. A cannon ball explodes into the bow. Shrapnel falls like hail. The *San Paulo* rocks to her side. I grab the mast and brace. She's going to tip!

But the ship steadies. She regains the wind and makes speed.

"Drop all sails! Charlie, check the damage. Make sure the hole is above the water line. Gunther, man the wheel. Get us out of this bay. Isabelle, come with me. We're going to fire back."

Isabelle and I run below deck. Gunther releases the other sails. Never in my brief time as captain has the *San Paulo* sailed under the full power of its three sails. The white cloth glows in the moonlight, as if she's a ghost ship.

Another cannon ball rips across the deck, carving a canyon in front of me and Isabelle. I hold up my arms to protect my face. Several splinters lodge themselves in my forearm. A thick piece of timber slams into my stomach, knocking the breath from me. But otherwise, it causes no harm.

"Isabelle are you alright?"

A splinter cut across Isabelle's cheek. Another gashed from her forehead to nose, but somehow it missed her eye. Blood drips from both wounds.

She wipes her face and composes herself. "I'll deal with it later! We've got to do something about their cannons. We can't keep taking hits like this!" She opens the hatch to the gun deck. It's dark down there. I pause. I consider the cannon fire shredding into the ship. Isabelle, tired of waiting, goes first into the dark.

The cannon doors open with a thick clunk.

A third cannon ball slams into the stern of the ship. Probably crashed right through the captain's cabin. The ship swivels—the impact of the cannon ball threw us off course. Unless Gunther is careful at the wheel, another shot like that could run us aground. If that happens, we're dead in the water.

All I can do is go below deck, shoot at the cannons on the fortress wall, and hope Gunther keeps the *San Paulo* sailing straight.

All the cannons are loaded. They've been begging to be fired since they gobbled up their powder and cannon balls. Now they have their chance.

The blood dripping from Isabelle's face shines like glass. "You aim. I'll fire."

I rush to the first cannon and heave myself against the pitted iron. Grunting, I aim it toward the fortress. I lay my cheek to the cold metal and sight along the barrel. Captain Solway is positioned directly in the barrel's sights.

A cannon ball splashes into the water outside the cannon hatch where I'm working. Water droplets splash through the hatch and wet my face. No impact—the ship doesn't jerk so the ball's aim was off. If it had been a bit higher, it would've blown through the gun deck.

"Have you got the cannon sighted or are you waiting for a written declaration of war to return fire?" Isabelle asks.

I step back from the cannon. "Light it."

She sets fire to the fuse at the rear of the cannon. The flame licks down the fuse and ignites the sack of gunpowder inside, firing the cannon. My ears ring at the sound of the blast. I flinch as the cannon recoils.

"Well? Did we hit them, or do I need to aim next time?"

Stones from the fortress wall crumble to the sand. The shot decimated one of their cannon hatches. A cannon and its two operators tumble from the breech.

That's a little less cannon fire to deal with.

"Direct hit," I say.

"Good, to the next cannon then."

In the distance, Captain Solway stands at the top of the fortress. He's propped against one of the long cannons aimed at our ship. I should have put a dagger in his chest.

All the fortress fires are extinguished. Solway waves his good arm like a man mad at the sky. The fortress is intact—save a little fire damage, the crumbled door, and the cannon we blew up. Captain Solway is determined to not be the British Captain who allowed the *San Paulo* to escape Long Rock.

He yells, "Fire!"

Explosions cut through the wet night, clacking the air as the balls fly. The ship jolts, a cannon ball found its mark somewhere. All I know is it didn't hit the gun deck.

We'll never make it out of the bay at this rate. The *San Paulo* is riddled with cannon fire. I don't see water at my feet so she's not sinking. Yet.

For our next shot, I line the cannon's muzzle with Captain Solway's head. Not out of spite, or for my own survival, but for my father's sake. It's to ensure this man can offer no report or reprise against my father. It will never be known that Admiral William Higgins was robbed of the king's treasure by his own son.

I check the sights one more time. Captain Solway's head, made miniature by the great distance, sits on the muzzle of the cannon.

"Ready to fire."

Isabelle touches the flame to the fuse. The cannon cracks in a hot blast of air. The ball shoots across the black water. It jams into the fortress wall beneath Captain Solway's feet.

The wall crumbles. Stones fall to the beach below, cratering the sand. Captain Solway staggers. He's still unsteady from being shot. As the wall beneath him crumbles, he trips and falls with the rubble.

Several cannons tumble from the tower. They fall like punches and crush his body.

Without the harsh orders of Captain Solway, there's nothing left to keep the soldiers at their posts. They stand down. *If the San Paulo wants to destroy a godforsaken fortress in the middle of nowhere, by God, let her.*

The cannon fire stops.

I collapse onto a stack of cloth. My whole body is drained from aiming the cannons—and from everything else that's happened since this time last night. Can it have only been one day since we stole the *San Paulo*?

Isabelle slumps down next to me. Together we enjoy the cool air blowing through the hatches. Her face is coated in grime and sweat and blood.

My back aches, but I stand and dip a rag in the barrel of water reserved for putting out fires. I give Isabelle the damp rag. I return to the barrel and splash water in my face. That's when I notice the splinters in both my arms. Gunther will have a time pulling all of those out. I groan and throw myself onto the sacks.

Isabelle gently wipes the blood from her nose. Some will say her face is forever ruined—that it's scorned. Scars will form across her eye and cheek. But she'll wear those scars like she does a sword belt, naturally, and as though she were born with them.

"Look." Isabelle points toward the window.

Before we lose sight of the bay, I see a horde of men leaving the fortress. They're doing more than escaping. From their gait, you can tell they have a mission. At the head of the pack is my father.

Relief pours over me like gentle rain. My father survived the decimation of the fortress. He, with his crew at his back, dart for the *Endurance*.

Moving like men with purpose, they throw themselves aboard the ship. They swing from ropes and drop sails. At the helm stands my father, looking at us with his spyglass. He's probably inspecting the damage wrought upon my ship.

He passes from my view. Regardless of his intent, whether he's chasing me or ensuring my safe passage, he won't catch us. With our sails in the full wind, we'll leave the fortress behind—my father with it. But he'll be fine. His career will be intact with the death of Captain Solway. I have peace that—besides harming his reputation by stealing the treasure —I didn't cost my father his livelihood.

I should go about the ship, inspect the damage, plug holes, and plot a course with Charlie. But all I can do is lay my head down next to Isabelle, exhausted.

20

THE DAMASCUS

"WAKE UP, CAPTAIN." GUNTHER LEANS OVER ME AND NUDGES MY shoulder with his rough fingers. I shield my eyes from his lantern. He lifts my arm and examines my skin. "I know you're tired, but we need to see to these splinters before they fester."

He pulls a short knife from his apron and sharpens the edge on a whetstone. Using the side of the knife and his thumb, he pulls the shards of wood from my arms. One by one, the damp splinters falls to the floor. My arms bleed.

The wounds sting as Gunther scrubs them. He wraps a clean piece of cloth around my arms. The blood soaks in, making the surface a dull pink. The bandage holds, and my arms feel much better.

"I best see to Isabelle as well." He gently shakes her shoulder. "M'lady."

She jerks to wakefulness, as if she's ready to run or fight or stick a cutlass in someone's gut. Slowly, she remembers where she is, and her muscles relax. She touches her face and feels the crusty wounds.

"I'll fix you right up," Gunther says.

Before he uses a wet cloth to wash the dried blood, he lifts her chin and turns her face side to side, examining the wounds in the low light. It's the same way she first examined him. The water from the rag loosens the blood and wipes it away. Two wrinkled lacerations stretch across Isabelle's right eye and left cheek. Once the blood is wiped away, he wraps a clean cloth around her head, winding it over her cheek where the cuts are the worst.

"There, good as new." He pats her shoulder.

"Thank you." She feels the bandages.

"Of course. Now, James, I suppose you'll be wanting to see your treasure." Gunther motions for us to follow him to the cargo hold.

Supplies, cannon balls, and wood are scattered from the fortress battle. Yet the cargo hold, by some miracle, remained intact. No damage other than several overturned crates of gold.

In the hold the treasure looks larger than it did ashore the island. Gunther pushes me forward, like he wants me to feel the coins clink beneath my feet. I kneel and take a handful of treasure. The gold pieces feel light, like sand, as they strain through my fingers and clatter into piles. The treasure heap shimmers like a sun we stole and stashed in our hull.

So much gold.

And it belongs to the four of us.

"We did alright," Gunther says as he kicks an overturned treasure chest.

"Aye." I take an onyx ring from the pile and slide it on my finger. "We did good."

Too much is left to be done tonight for us to bathe in the glow of our treasure. As much as I'd like to spend the night swimming in the piles of gold, there is more danger afoot.

We've won our riches. Now comes the dangerous part—keeping it. I've read enough stories to know most adventurers win treasure only to lose it because they lowered their guard. I don't intend to be that sort of fool.

"We should plot our course," Gunther says.

The three of us climb the ladder to the main deck. This time last night, we were preparing the ship for our intercept with the *Endurance*. The poor *San Paulo*—mutilated, riddled with cannon fire, and sailed by the four who kidnapped her. If she could talk, she'd beg to be scuttled.

But she's got a long journey before that. She's got to get us to Africa.

I step across the ravine carved by a cannon ball. Splinters protrude. Moonlight leaks into the crew's quarters below. The figurehead and the bowsprit are gone. The sails once connected to that mast writhe like a dying butterfly.

On the bridge of the ship, Charlie waits for us with his sea charts weighed down by heavy shards of wood. He's holding a sextant to the sky.

Gashes run across his face. Something cut through his shirt and grazed his arm, but otherwise he fared well during the sea battle.

"How's the leak, Charlie?" Gunther asks as he steps onto the bridge.

"Not as bad as I first thought. I've got it mostly patched. A little water's still coming in, so we'll probably be bailing all the way to Africa, but the *San Paulo* should limp her way there."

Gunther leans against the railing and looks relieved. The leak must've been worrying him.

"Anything else to report?" I ask.

"The Captain's cabin was blasted to bits, but it's far enough above the water line that it doesn't matter. The bow may as well be gone. Without the front sail, we'll lose some speed, but we can manage. Oh, we've also got a canyon cut through the middle of the deck, but I assume you can see that. If we encounter any bad weather, any passing swell will pour in. But like I said, we should be able to hobble our way to Africa. What's the name of the settlement? Côte da Seal?"

"La Côte du Ciel." Isabelle steps toward him. "It might not be on your sea maps. It's a small colony." She points to a spot along the African coast line. "It's about right there."

"I'll plot our course, put us to the wind, and then we should get some rest for the night. Oh, and James, there's something else. We're being followed." He hands me a spy glass and points to the horizon.

At the edge of what can be seen through the spy glass, outlined in the setting moon, is the *Endurance*.

She's far enough off that she could never catch us, but she still struggles to keep up. What is my father doing? Is he chasing me or ensuring my safe passage to the Atlantic?

It's hard to know, but he won't be able to keep up through the night. We'll lose him by morning.

Knowing the truth about my father brought me peace, but like he said—I have to make my own way in the world. Running off with this treasure is my destiny, I imagine. My father will understand. He may have lost his treasure, but I left him another in the note on his desk.

Charlie plots our course, turns the wheel, and checks the sextant one more time. He interrogates the stars to ensure they're telling him the truth. Once he's satisfied with their answers, he says "goodnight" and heads below deck. He doesn't bother taking the stairs, he jumps through the hole cut across the deck by the cannon fire.

"I'll leave you two pups to chat." Gunther takes his leave. Isabelle and I are left alone on the bridge of the ship.

"I'm sorry for considering to ransom you."

She isn't looking at me. "You're a fool."

I'm not sure why, but I say, "I am a pirate."

"As am I, but I didn't ransom you off to your father when he found you aboard the *Endurance*. I could've squeezed some extra gold from him. I could've alerted him to your presence even before you got yourself caught. I could've just left you to rot in Long Rock, but I didn't. We were loyal to you—even me. And you have no right to my loyalty."

"I know."

"So, who are you loyal to, James?"

"To my family."

She rears back, thinking that I was referring to my father.

I clarify. "To my new family. To Charlie, to Gunther, to you."

"Do you mean it?"

"Yes."

"I'm going to trust you." Even before the bandages, her face was hard to read. But I sense deep sincerity and a hint of forgiveness in her eyes.

I hadn't noticed before, but she's holding something—my old hat. She swaggers over and plops it on my head.

———

In the morning, sunlight slips through the gaping hole on the deck of the ship. I hear the churn of the ocean and taste salty air. The ship creaks— probably due to the instability caused by all the damages—but Charlie said she would get us across the Atlantic. Albeit barely.

Charlie grunts and rolls over in his hammock while Gunther snores. They probably won't wake for several hours.

My arms are as stiff as my legs and back. I sit up and touch my bare feet to the splintery floor. Clothes are set out beside me—my white shirt, pants, heavy leather boots, thick weapon belt to put over my shoulder, and my captain's hat.

I quickly dress and go to the next barrack where Isabelle slept. She's not in her hammock. She must have gone above deck to inspect the ship's damage in the daylight.

Isabelle slams into me as I climb toward the deck. She's dressed, has her cutlasses at her sides, and a bandana around her head to tame her hair, but she's afraid. "James, we need to wake Gunther and Charlie. Now!"

"Why? What's going on?" I follow her through the ship's barracks to where Gunther and Charlie sleep.

Her movements are hurried, almost panicked. "No time. We need to get them above deck."

She throws Charlie out of his hammock. He snaps to wakefulness. He scampers about the floor, hand reaching for a pistol or cutlass or something to use as a weapon because he thinks we're under attack. After he regains his senses, he stands up, only wearing his under garments. He rubs his head. "What was that for?"

"No time to explain. Put your clothes on and get to the bridge. We've got a problem." She shakes Gunther's shoulder vigorously and he stirs. "Gunther, wake up and get dressed."

Isabelle rushes up the ladder to the deck.

Gunther rubs his forehead. He checks the sun through the hole in the ceiling. "What's gotten into her?"

Charlie puts his shirt on backwards. He ties the front of his pants as he smacks his lips. He stumbles to the water barrel.

I don't wait on Charlie and Gunther. Whatever has got Isabelle on edge must be bad. I push through the rows of hammocks and follow Isabelle.

She stands at the bridge, spy glass to her eye, frowning. At the end of the spyglass, to our port side, is an approaching ship with grey sails and a black flag.

My heart sputters—a pirate ship. They have the favorable wind. We've got to adjust our course quickly before they catch us. Even then, they'll still be faster.

Charlie and Gunther stagger through the deck hatch. Gunther's trained eye instantly notices the ship in the distance. Then his face goes pale when he sees the black flag.

"Pirates," he mutters.

"James, hurry up!" Isabelle yells at me from the bridge of the ship.

I run toward the bridge. "Charlie, loose every bit of sail cloth we have. We stand no chance in a fight. We have to run."

Charlie climbs to the topsail to set loose our only reefed sail.

Isabelle hands me the spy glass. "Look."

Through the spyglass, the ship in the distance is clear. The flag, four skulls cooking over a flame, belongs to Captain Marcello of the *Damascus* —the life-long rival of Captain Rodriguez. At least a hundred men scurry about the deck like a hive of bees, all ready to sting. How did he get so many men? That's twice the number the *Damascus* should carry.

Gunther must have recognized the flag too because he murmurs, "God help us."

Isabelle nudges me. "Look at the bridge."

I pan the spyglass up. Standing at the wheel of the ship, face twisted as though Satan lives in him, staring back at me through the spyglass, checking my features to ensure he has found the object of his revenge, is Captain Rodriguez de Medina.

21

SAVAGES

CHARLIE GRIMACES AT THE RAPID APPROACH OF THE *DAMASCUS*. He's leaned over the side of the ship, an hour glass in one hand; a spool of knots in the other. He drops the knot line in the water to check our speed. "We can't out run them. I've let loose every sail we have. It isn't enough. They've got the wind. I gained us a few knots, but they'll catch us before night fall."

The *Damascus* moves like a shark closing in on a wounded fish. Hundreds of angry pirates are on board. All of them ready to kill us for marooning them on that godforsaken beach. Apparently, our actions were enough to move Captain Marcello to aid his rival, Captain Rodriguez. It gives a bad name to pirates everywhere when three adolescents can steal a ship, and a king's treasure, with immunity.

Charlie is right; we'll never out run them. They're moving too fast, have too strong a wind in their sails, and too strong a will. They'll catch us, even if we were to escape today. They'll hunt us all over the New World. Only in Africa would we have been safe, but we'll never make it there. All that's left to do is find a white flag—if Captain Rodriguez even kept one—and surrender.

No. We've come too far, won too much. I shake my head, pushing the thought of surrender away. The gold is ours.

If we were clever enough to steal it, we're clever enough to keep it.

"How long until they come within firing range?" I ask.

Charlie looks at the approaching ship. "About an hour."

"Alright, we need to make a plan."

"What are we making a plan for?" Isabelle doesn't turn to face me. She's watching the *Damascus* approach. All of her gold and freedom is slipping through her fingers. Captain Rodriguez will kill Charlie, Gunther, and I, but Isabelle—she won't be killed. He'll lock her up and ransom her off to her father. To Isabelle, a cage is worse than death.

"We'll make a plan to fight." I say.

Gunther rubs his head like an old man tired of playing a young man's game. Charlie looks to the sky, wondering why this sort of thing always falls into his lap. Isabelle looks hopeful.

But like me, she saw the horde of pirates aboard the *Damascus*. Hundreds of them—dirty, armed, and angry. She saw the look of blood in Captain Rodriguez's eyes.

I have no idea how Rodriguez managed to get off that beach, make it to a port, locate Captain Marcello, and then convince him to chase us. All of that, in less than a day. Yet I'm not surprised. A man like Rodriguez will do anything to enact revenge.

"Gunther, stay above deck and keep an eye on the *Damascus*. Make sure she doesn't get too close."

"Aye, I'll stand up here and watch my clock tick down." Gunther looks over his shoulder and shudders. He told me once that Rodriguez strips mutineers naked, covers them in honey, and ties them to a beach full of hermit crabs. "Hope you three come up with something good."

I motion for Charlie and Isabelle to follow.

The captain's cabin is a wreck of wood splinters, paper from ripped books, and shards from relics, tribal shields, and stone cuttings Rodriguez collected. The cannon ball blew straight threw. It knocked one gaping hole in the port side, and another through to the starboard. Sun shines in through both holes, giving us plenty of light to work.

At the center of the desolation sits Rodriguez's antique desk. Compared to everything else, the desk isn't much worse for wear. A few new scratches and a gash or two, but it's perfectly intact. It must be made of the same stuff as Captain Rodriguez.

I brush away the fragments of pottery and wood shards. They clatter to the floor as Isabelle pushes an elephant tusk, shot in half, out of the way to reach the chest of sea charts. She unrolls a map across the desk. Charlie points to our current location.

I run my fingers across the old, crinkled map, feeling the islands and atolls of the Caribbean. Open ocean surrounds our position. To the West are a few British controlled islands. To the North is the strait at Key Largo.

"Charlie, could we make it to either of these places before the *Damascus* catches us?" I point to the strait. And then to the British islands.

"We could make it to strait, no question about it. It isn't far, but as for the islands, we wouldn't make it by night fall. Those are in British controlled waters so there's a chance we might bump into a warship or friendly merchant if we fly a British flag."

"We should make for the strait," Isabelle says as she looks at the map. "We could lose them there."

Even on the map, the strait is narrow. Shipwrecks are marked from its entrance to its exit. On the map, the entrance is guarded by a sea monster.

"Do you know how many ships have been lost in that strait?" Charlie says. "More than I dare count. Massive coral reefs grow there. They'll slice into the hull of a ship if you're not careful to miss them. As undermanned as we are, we would never make it."

"Then just what do you suggest we do?"

"I have no idea! We're in the middle of nowhere with a horde of pirates behind us. We're already slow and our ship barely floats. I hate to say this, but we might need to abandon ship. We can all slip off in a jolly boat and leave the *San Paulo* sailing in another direction. They won't notice us slip away and they'll follow the *San Paulo*. A few days of hard rowing, and we could make it to shore. We might even be able to keep a small chest of gold. What do you think, James?"

I had only been catching bits of their conversation. The map has another secret left. It has to. The British islands are our best chance. If we can reach British controlled waters, all we need is to pass a willing ship.

My father once told me a story about Indians. He was protecting the plantations near Charleston. His unit was assigned to hunt a tribe of warriors that lived deep in the interior. The Indians used a tactic my father and his men weren't familiar with—hit and run.

Repetitively, the Indians sprung from the trees, killed a few men, and then led my father's unit deeper into the wilderness. The Indians were baiting them. In the end, the Indians led my father's unit into the heart of a large, violent tribe's territory. The unit was massacred. Only my father survived.

The Indians my father was chasing were out manned, out gunned, and should have lost. Instead, they led my father's unit into a trap.

We will be the Indians.

If we slowed the *Damascus* down, we could make it to British waters. Our tribe is too small to fight them, but surely there's a British warship itching to sink the *Damascus*. All we must do is lead the *Damascus* to them.

Hit and run.

Lead and deceive.

Like savages.

Charlie slams his fist onto the desk. "We're not going through the strait!"

"It's our only chance!" Isabelle counters. "We've risked too much to walk away with only a crate of gold. All of the treasure is ours!"

"Isabelle is right," I say. "We're not surrendering our treasure, not a single piece goes into their filthy hands. I think we should fight them."

Charlie and Isabelle turn to me, disbelief on both their faces.

"James, how?" Isabelle asks.

"We'll play a game of hit and run. We don't have to sink them to beat them. We just have to slow them down. If we can slow them enough to make it to the British waters near these islands," I point to the map, "we can hope to cross paths with a British patrol ship."

Charlie shakes his head. "You have a good way to slow them down? Because last time I checked none of us are a god able to control the wind."

"They have the better wind, you're right. But because they are the attacking ship, we have a defensive advantage. When they get close, we'll swing around and broadside them. If our shots are accurate, they'll rip through their ship, bow to stern. That should slow them down. If they get too close again, we'll fire with our port cannons. We'll need to reload the cannons we fired at Long Rock, but otherwise all the cannons are still loaded."

Isabelle shakes her head. "If we miss, they'll have a clear path to us. We won't be able to build up enough speed to out run them again."

"You won't miss," I say.

She smiles, but then quickly scowls, returning to the argument at hand. "Your plan leaves too much to chance."

"I leave nothing to chance," I say.

"Your plan is hedged on crossing paths with a British ship. They patrol those waters, but what if we don't encounter one?"

"We will."

"No, we need to make for the strait. It relies only on us and doesn't count on finding a British ally."

Despite the tension, Charlie laughs. "Both plans will probably get us killed. And since neither of you want to give my plan a chance—which is the most survivable one, by the way—let's flip for it. Both are equally suicidal. James, pull out that lucky coin of yours. Let's see how lucky it really is."

"Fine," Isabelle says.

I pull out my Spanish doubloon. The face of the Spanish king glimmers in the sun pouring in through the fragmented walls. For a second, I swear the face is smiling. It's been lucky so far. Maybe it has just enough left to help us survive. "Heads we engage, try to slow them down, and make for the British islands. Tails, we traverse the strait."

"Alright," Isabelle says.

With the tip of my thumb, I toss the coin. It spins into the air. I catch it in the palm of my hand and slap it to my wrist.

Charlie and Isabelle lean in. I lift my hand. The coin is face up.

We fight the *Damascus*.

"It's settled then," Charlie says.

Isabelle grunts. "Yeah, it's settled. We're going to die."

I ignore her comment. "We'll shoot our first volley when they get too close for comfort. We'll give no advance warning. I'll swing the wheel and fire all the cannons. Gunther and Isabelle will be below deck. You'll need to fire them quickly because we can't stay broadside for long or we'll slow down too much. Charlie will man the sails. I'll stand by the wheel. We need to get above deck and fill Gunther in."

Charlie chuckles as he leaves the Captain's cabin. "Yeah, he's going to love this one."

Isabelle stops me as I pass the door out of the captain's cabin. She points to the pocket where I stow my coin. She crosses her arms. "I thought you never left anything to chance?"

"I don't. It's a lucky coin."

22

THOSE WHO LOVE YOU WILL STILL LOVE YOU

AS THE SUN LOWERS, THE *DAMASCUS* APPROACHES. ALL OF HER SAILS swell with wind. They carry the ship across the ocean. At this range, I see Captain Rodriguez standing on the bridge. His fists are balled tight, as if he's imagining them squeezed around my neck.

Captain Marcello stands at the wheel, looking dull in the glow of Captain Rodriguez—who's wearing his flamboyant red coat with the gold cuffs. Not to mention his feathered hat. Captain Marcello, however, wears simple black pants, a loose blue shirt, a weapon belt with saber and pistol. All that distinguishes him from his crew is his Captain's hat. I've never met the man, but I've heard stories. He's more subdued than Rodriguez —not as much of a showman—but he is cunning and cruel and smart.

He probably thinks this will be an easy spoil. No matter how this ends, he's wrong.

From the gaping hole across the deck of my ship, I watch Isabelle and Gunther reload the cannons. Gunther struggles with a cannon ball. Isabelle checks the sighting along the barrel.

After they load the cannons, they run a long, braided fuse to the main deck. Charlie picks it up and runs it to the bridge. He hands it off to me and I tie it to the railing by the wheel.

Isabelle fastens the fuse's other end to the ship's store of gunpowder.

Come what may, Rodriguez isn't getting the treasure.

Charlie climbs about in the upper rigging of the ship, checking the ropes one last time before we engage. He'll maintain a vantage point atop the sails to adjust for changing winds.

I look back. The *Damascus* is near enough.

"Gunther, Isabelle, are you ready?" I call down through the deck.

"Aye, Captain," Gunther says.

Isabelle is silent, but she looks me in the eyes. Even from the distance, I see her resolve. She'll either fly away from this like a phoenix, her wings spread wide in a blaze, or she'll be the blaze.

I adjust my captain's hat. "Prepare for combat."

With all of my weight, I lean hard on the wheel, turning us portside. The ship comes about to broadside the *Damascus*. The *San Paulo* jerks beneath my feet. We lose momentum as we come off the wind. The wounded ship groans in protest from all her broken joints, but she turns. Our row of cannons face the *Damascus*.

I pat the wheel. "Not much longer. Just see us through a little more and we'll give you a proper burial."

With the spyglass, I scan the deck of the *Damascus*. Through the speckled glass, I see the shocked faces of Captain Marcello and Captain Rodriguez. Their mouths hang open. They hadn't been expecting this. At this range, cannon fire will cause monumental damage.

They snap from their daze and bark orders.

But it's too late for them to avoid our cannon fire. I turn to my crew and cry, "Charlie, adjust the sails to catch the new wind! Isabelle, Gunther, fire when ready!"

A single cannon booms beneath me. The ball rips into the *Damascus*. It runs the whole length of the port side. The hole is barely above the water line. As the sea ebbs and flows, water will pour in, eventually causing the ship to lean, and if unchecked, sink.

Another cannon shot rings, crunching right down the middle of their ship. Wood shards fly as the cannon ball tears the deck, bow to stern.

"Two direct hits! Keeping firing!" I yell.

Captain Rodriguez seems to be stunned, as if he can't believe three young devils are outsmarting him, again. Even now, he's probably considering the possibility that we're possessed. Some demons are better left alone.

But Captain Marcello seems to be more cognizant. He grabs the wheel and jerks it down, turning his ship so that they can return fire.

A cannon blast explodes into the gun deck of the *Damascus*. She shows her starboard side. All her cannon doors face us. Twenty cannons pop out like twenty rifles at an execution.

"Prepare for impact! Charlie, adjust the sails. Get us moving—"

Enemy fire rips into the stern of the ship. I shiver when I realize how close that shot was to me. I lean over the side to check the damage. The hole is barely above the water. If that shot had been slightly lower, it would have been fatal. Water splashes in as the ship bobs.

Another cannon ball skitters across the deck. Gunther and Isabelle block their heads from the shrapnel.

"Are you okay?" I yell.

"Get us out of here, James! We can't keep taking hits like this," Isabelle yells.

As she speaks, Charlie adjusts the sails and the *San Paulo* picks up speed. We move from the *Damascus*'s line of fire.

That doesn't stop them from trying to hit us. Cannon balls splash into the water off the *San Paulo*'s stern.

The *Damascus* moves sluggishly. Having turned to engage us, she lost her wind. She'll have to readjust. Releasing a deep breath, I steady myself. As mad as that was, it worked. Because of the surprise, we bought some time.

Charlie swings down from the upper rigging. "Orders, Captain?"

"Check the damage."

He rushes off to inspect the new holes and to make sure no fires were lit. As he runs down the stairs, Isabelle and Gunther climb up. Gunther's eyes are wide as if he's amazed he's still alive. "Never would have thought that would work."

Isabelle doesn't look so surprised. She looks as if she knew we would win. Instead, she is impatient. "How long before the *Damascus* closes in on us again? We won't have the element of surprise this time."

Aboard the *Damascus*, the men are frantically scurrying about the ship. They're adjusting the sails to catch new wind and give chase, but they're far away.

Isabelle frowns. "We're not making good enough speed. I don't think we can make it into British waters."

"We'll make it." I turn my lucky coin between my fingers.

Charlie rushes up the stairs to the bridge, out of breath. He joins us by the wheel.

"Report," I say.

"We're still floating but took heavy damage. All the holes are above the waterline, but if we make any sharp turns, they'll dip below, and we'll take on water. We've lost all versatility."

"So we can't fire another volley?" Isabelle asks.

"No."

The three of us are silent. We all know what that means.

Behind us, the *Damascus* gains speed faster than we anticipated. She's almost to the distance where we fired our volley. We stand no chance of making it to British waters.

The wind carries the war cries of the pirates mad with rage. I swear I distinctly hear Rodriguez's curses.

Flint stones rattle in my pocket. A small torch lays by my feet. I kneel down and light it. The time has come to ignite the fuse leading to the gunpowder. Charlie, Gunther, and Isabelle nod as in agreement. No one needs to say anything. We lost, but we're going to take our last revenge. We'll scuttle the *San Paulo* now, over deep water.

Isabelle steps between me and Gunther. She grabs each of our hands with a slight squeeze. She stands with her head high, the free breeze in her hair. Her hand is warm and covered in soot and grit. Gunther puts his free hand on Charlie's shoulder and pulls him close to us.

"Ready?" I ask.

"Aye." Isabelle closes her eye.

I lower the torch to the fuse.

"Wait!" Gunther cries. "British colors to the East!"

A ship cuts across the water faster than I've ever seen a ship move. Its sails are full, and it moves with a purpose—as if it's mission was to intercept with us and the *Damascus*. As it nears, I see a man standing tall on the bridge. It's my father.

"It's the *Endurance*," Isabelle whispers. She lets go of Gunther and me. She moves to the railing to watch the British warship.

"Yes, it's the *Endurance*!" I toss the torch into the water. We should make our escape, but I want to watch the coming desolation.

The fully manned warship crests the waves with elegance. The British are the masters of the sea. Men climb up and down her masts, adjusting the sails, measuring their speed. Down below, they're loading the cannons.

Behind us, the *Damascus* sees its approaching doom. Through the spyglass, I see Captain Marcello waving his arms in a blind panic. He orders his men to adjust course. Even laden with two crews, the *Damascus* will be decimated.

The *Damascus* adjusts her course, ends her pursuit of us, and flees. They are too late.

Within minutes the *Endurance* is parallel to her. Her gun deck doors open and her cannons crack. Cannon balls blast across the ocean with the accuracy only the British Navy has mastered.

The *Damascus* returns fire, but her cannons are indistinguishable from the war drum of fire from the *Endurance*.

The *Endurance* fires volley after volley. The cannon balls rip into the *Damascus*'s naked side, thrashing through the old wood, throwing men overboard, setting the ship ablaze. The volleys continue even after the *Damascus* stops fighting back. Today it seems my father isn't taking prisoners.

In an explosion of iron, wood, and flesh, the *Damascus* slowly sinks. But my father continues to fire, ensuring that the *Damascus* makes her way to the bottom of the ocean.

Isabelle touches my shoulder. "We should go now, James."

"You're right. Charlie, plot us a course for Africa. We're headed to La Côte du Ciel."

I turn the wheel after Charlie consults the sea charts. The *San Paulo* gets underway with a strong wind pulling us East. That wind will carry us across the Atlantic and to our new home.

Above us, Charlie climbs the rigging, happy and in his element.

Gunther stretches. "Well, this has been an eventful few days for an old man. I think I'll go lay down. Don't wake me unless we're being attacked by a kraken. And only then if we're losing." He heads below deck.

Isabelle and I are the only ones who look back. The *Endurance* surveys the *Damascus*'s wreckage. My hope is that Rodriguez died as the ship caught fire. Because if not, he'll swim across the Atlantic to kill us. But even if by some miracle he survives the wreck, he has to survive my father.

"Look." Isabelle nudges my shoulder.

Through the smoke, across the sea littered with flotsam, my father waves goodbye.

I wave back.

23

THE COAST OF HEAVEN

THE COAST OF AFRICA IS GREEN, AND THE AIR IS WARM. WIND carries the songs of savage tribes from inland. Dolphins swim in the pristine water. It took us three months to get here. Partly because Charlie got us lost, and partly because the *San Paulo* barely floats. But we have finally arrived at La Côte du Ciel.

Charlie, Isabelle, and I are alone aboard the *San Paulo*. As we wait for Gunther to return, we survey the port town. He took a jolly boat into town to hire a cart. The driver will meet us in an obscure bay a few miles North of here.

"I want that one." Charlie points to a mansion sitting on the hilltop, the jungle to its back. It's white and built in the typical filigree and finery of French architecture.

"Well, I want that one." Isabelle points to a smaller mansion perched on a sea cliff.

"Okay, okay, fine. I'll buy the one back there and you can have your little death trap on the cliff," Charlie says.

Me—I'll be happy with any of them. Regardless of Charlie's joking, we'll all live in the same house, happily, never setting foot on the sea again. We'll settle down. If the urge strikes in ten or fifteen years—once the *Endurance* scandal dies down—we'll go some place else. But I could stay in La Côte du Ciel forever.

I don't understand why the French nobility scorned this town. It has a raw beauty, yet it's tamed enough for the conveniences of a city—a blacksmith, baker, grocer, and printer. Nevertheless, it's still wild enough to know the jungle. It's perfect.

Gunther rows to the *San Paulo* and then climbs aboard. We lug him over the railing.

"I hired a nice young Frenchman. He's a merchant who deals with horses, I think. He didn't speak particularly good English, but I told him to bring a big cart."

Charlie climbs the rigging and lets loose some sail. We make for the prearranged resting ground. A pod of dolphins swim alongside us—the *San Paulo*'s funeral procession. Once we're underway, Charlie climbs down, locates his violin from the rubble, and rosins his bow. He plays the *San Paulo* a final dirge.

The bay we chose is secluded. A waterfall from deep in the jungle flows into the salt water. I know the *San Paulo* is just a ship, but Charlie wanted to find her a nice grave.

Our man with the cart is waiting for us as we glide into the bay. He brought a large cart, a strong horse, and no questions.

Charlie and Gunther load treasure into a boat. After a few crates, the jolly boat is ready to tip.

"This might take a few trips," Charlie says.

A few trips turn into fifteen. The Frenchman's eyes grow wider with each crate Gunther and Charlie ferry. I check the cargo hold. Coins are scattered across the floor and some crates sit in the corner. Should only take two more trips. Charlie and Gunther can handle that without me.

I climb down below with Isabelle. We run a long fuse to the mounds of gunpowder for the scuttling.

People will see, hear, and feel the explosion for miles. Instead of decimating his enemies, Captain Rodriguez's gun powder stash will blow up his ship.

"A shame, really," Isabelle says.

"What?"

"Scuttling the *San Paulo*. What if we want to be pirates again?"

I laugh. "If the itch hits you, I'll help you steal another ship—an even better ship."

"Promise?"

"I promise."

I call to the deck above. "Gunther, have you and Charlie gotten all the gold?"

"Every piece of it," Gunther says. "We just loaded the last boat. There's room for the two of you if you want to light the fuse and come on."

"Be right there." I hand Isabelle two flint stones. "Want to do the honor?"

She refuses them. "No, you've earned this."

I clink the stones and the spark catches flame. It crackles along the slow burning fuse that leads to the gunpowder. "Let's go."

Isabelle and I hurriedly climb above deck. We load into the boat with Charlie and Gunther. I look back at the *San Paulo*, ready for it to blow any second now.

"Row faster, Charlie," Isabelle says.

The *San Paulo* explodes. She breaks in half and scatters wood into the air. The shards fall like jungle rain. Pages from books float through the air like burning leaves. The two halves of our relieved ship sink into the bay. The fire tries to escape its fate by climbing the sails, but soon even the highest mast is below the water's surface. The *San Paulo* will forever be hidden.

Charlie cries. But he looks at the gold to remind himself it was worth it. Charlie, I've found, gets attached easily.

Sand crunches beneath the boat as we row ashore. I help Gunther and Charlie stack the treasure onto the cart. Because the chests are stacked higher than my head, Charlie climbs on top to load the last few. So much gold.

The Frenchman doesn't offer to help. He only stands there, dumbfounded.

He didn't ask where the gold came from, why the ship looked like it had gone to hell and back, or why we were scuttling it. The Frenchman didn't ask any questions. Gunther hands the man a sack of gold so heavy that his arms dip. Isabelle whispers in French, telling him to keep this our little secret.

The Frenchman looks up from the bag of gold. He replies to Isabelle.

"What did he say?" I ask.

"He said, 'Your secrets will share my grave.'"

———

Gunther is now Count Dubois and Isabelle is his daughter. Even with the fresh scars across her face, Isabelle plays the role of a high-born daughter well. She's convincing enough to counter Gunther's lack of decorum.

Charlie and I are their lowly servants. Isabelle dressed us in rags.

As for Gunther, Isabelle combed his hair, shaved his face, and dressed him in a fine blue suit and powdered wig. Gunther isn't happy playing dress up again, but he looks like a Count. Isabelle straightens his wig before we enter the mansion we want to buy.

We settled for the one on the sea cliff.

The real-estate officer of the colony waits for us. He's dressed in fine clothes—a black suit with a ruffled collar. He's a typical Frenchman— narrow eyes and a long nose held high. "Bonjour, mes amis. Comment allez-vous ce bon jour?"

Gunther looks confused. However, he responds with the little French Isabelle managed to teach him. "Oui. Bonejur."

Charlie gives him a thumbs-up.

Isabelle handles the rest of the conversation. She explains that Count Doubois recently had a stroke. That was why they came to La Côte du Ciel—for peace and quiet.

I don't understand the conversation, but I can tell the real-estate officer is suspicious. His fingers wind tightly around the keys. His questions are massaged away by a nice sack of English gold. No need to make a fuss over why the new count of Côte du Ciel has blue eyes, blond hair, and fair skin, while his daughter is dark in every sense of the word. Or question why a French Count can't actually speak French. I like the French; they don't ask uncomfortable questions.

The real-estate officer tosses Isabelle the keys.

The mansion on the sea cliff is ours.

We run the halls of our new home. We roll on the beds, dirty the fine carpets, and rearrange the furniture. Gunther goes to inspect the kitchens. I think he enjoys cooking. Now he can cook for pleasure.

The mansion is painted blue and built in the old French style. Large windows open to the sea. The best part is the massive vault hidden beneath the parlor. It's large enough to hide our treasure.

We tire of running the endless corridors. Charlie, Isabelle, and I go explore the gardens. Tropical plants—native to this part of Africa—line winding paths and surround marble statues. Gunther joins us in the garden. He's carrying a tray of food he prepared in his new kitchen.

On the stone table Gunther sets fresh bread, braised meats, and vegetables. And one last bottle of rum saved from the *San Paulo*'s store room. We enjoy the meal together. The plants cast long shadows as the evening cools.

From our table, we listen to the ocean beat against the cliff.

After we finish eating, Gunther takes the tray, pats me on the shoulder, and says, "You're a good lad, James." He wanders back into our new mansion. "Still got the devil in you though."

"So, what do we do tomorrow?" Charlie asks as he lays back in the grass.

"Whatever we want," I say.

"I want to buy paintings for the library," Isabelle says.

"Well, I want us to go fishing," Charlie counters.

"You two can flip for it." I take my coin and toss it to Isabelle.

She catches it, holds it between her finger and thumb, and turns it. "It's a misprint. The king's face is on both sides. My father had an entire collection of these."

Charlie laughs. "All this time? You were making decisions with a two-sided doubloon."

I look toward Isabelle. "I never leave anything to chance." Isabelle gives me the coin. "I knew the right choice each time, but I wanted the luck. I suppose I don't need it anymore." I turn it in my hand one last time. I walk to the sea cliff's edge and toss the coin into the ocean.

Instantly, I regret it, but then realize it was just a coin—what it represents is tucked safely away. I don't need luck anymore and I don't need mementos. The memory of my father wasn't held in that coin. I hold the memory of my father.

A distant word meanders to my mind—peace. I am at ease, happy to have my treasure, and to know all my father did for me.

The *Endurance*'s gold was his final gift.

I smile when I think of him.

One day, my father will rustle through the papers on his desk at Long Rock. He'll notice a small scrap with my handwriting. He'll recognize it instantly because he taught me to write. On that paper, he'll see the words *La Côte du Ciel.* It might take many years, but he'll come to me. Not with a British warship, but on a private sloop. He may even bring Emily and my half-siblings with him. Someday, my father and I will meet again, here, on the Coast of Heaven.

Isabelle approaches me. The churning sea lulls. She touches my hand, but her eyes remain fixed on the waves.

THE END

———

Join Nathan's Mailing List and never miss a release:
www.nathansmithwriting.com/join

———

Don't miss out on your next favorite teen or new adult read!

Join the Fire & Ice mailing list
www.fireandiceya.com

THANK YOU FOR READING

Did you enjoy this book?

We invite you to leave a review at the website of your choice, such as Goodreads, Amazon, Barnes & Noble, etc.

DID YOU KNOW THAT LEAVING A REVIEW...

- Helps other readers find books they may enjoy.
- Gives you a chance to let your voice be heard.
- Gives authors recognition for their hard work.
- Doesn't have to be long. A sentence or two about why you liked the book will do.

ABOUT THE AUTHOR

 I've watched Muslims pray Asr, Buddhists kowtow before golden Buddhas, and Taoists leave snack cakes on the altar of their chosen deity. I've seen dragon boats move like water striders across Chinese lakes and I've sung Queen on karaoke night. In South Florida, I watched the Bush Garden fireworks every night for an entire summer while I sat on the hood of my truck thinking about God. I've jumped from a plane and eaten pancakes with a rocket scientist. I've thrown shells in the ocean as I watched the sun set on a deserted island. I worked as a Southern Baptist minister before coming to China to be an ESL teacher. I have since continued my writing and look forward to publishing more Young Adult novels. As for who I really am, I enjoy good coffee, saltwater fish keeping, canoeing, quiet places, good friends, and my wife Jessica.

Join Nathan's newsletter
www.nathansmithwriting.com/join

or Follow him online
www.nathansmithwriting.com

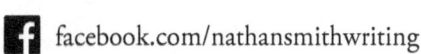 facebook.com/nathansmithwriting

www.ingramcontent.com/pod-product-compliance
Lightning Source LLC
Chambersburg PA
CBHW052143170626
46812CB00004B/1563